The
Collected
Poems of
KATHLEEN
RAINE

The Collected Poems of KATHLEEN RAINE

COUNTERPOINT
WASHINGTON, D.C.

Copyright © 2001 Kathleen Raine

Originally published in English by Golgonooza Press under the title:
The Collected Poems of Kathleen Raine
© Copyright 2000 Kathleen Raine

All rights reserved under international and Pan-American Copyright
Conventions. No part of this book may be used or reproduced in any manner
whatsoever without written permission from the Publisher, except in
the case of brief quotations embodied in critical articles and reviews.

Library of Congress Cataloging-in-Publication Data
Raine, Kathleen, 1908–
   [Poems. Selections]
   The collected poems of Kathleen Raine.
      p.   cm.
   ISBN 1-58243-135-3 (alk. paper)
   1. Imagination—Poetry.   I. Title.

PR6035.A37 A6 2000
821'.912—dc21
                                    00-064448

FIRST PRINTING

Jacket design by Dave Bullen
Typset by Colin Etheridge

Printed in the United States of America on acid-free paper that meets
the American National Standards Institute Z39-48 Standard

COUNTERPOINT
P.O. Box 65793
Washington, D.C. 20035-5793

Counterpoint is a member of the Perseus Books Group

10 9 8 7 6 5 4 3 2 1

Foreword

'A volume of Collected Poems is a poet's opportunity to discard work that should never have been published.' These words, written in 1956, open my Introduction to the volume of *Collected Poems* published in that year. They remain true, but nearly half a life-time has passed between 1956 and 2000, and the perspective has changed. The collection of 1956 represented the achievement of a 'young' poet, but now, in retrospect, represent the juvenilia of an old one.

It is nevertheless true that a writer's early work often contains the essence of the work that follows, a sort of map of that special vision. I see that from my first volume, *Stone and Flower*, I have omitted twenty-two poems, from *Living in Time* (my second) kept only fourteen. I have omitted poems from all my separate collections except *On a Deserted Shore*, which is a single poem.

There are it seems two kinds of poet, those who write their poems only once – like Coleridge, whose *Kubla Khan* and *The Rime of the Ancient Mariner* are unprecedented and unrepeatable. The other kind seems to draw on a certain kind of vision that remains constant. Among my contemporaries I find that David Gascoyne does not repeat himself. I seem to belong to the other class, who attempt to write the same poem many times, some versions being better than others; which to keep and which to leave out is often difficult to decide. Probably people who know my work well will disagree with some of my decisions, which are not indeed absolute judgments, but it hardly matters if some poems are a little better, others not quite so good. Throughout my life I have occasionally written a poem that has seemed self-generated and has emerged flawless, without a word to be changed and 'without labour or study' as Blake says of his own experience. In these poems I find a special quality, as of what would once have been described as 'inspiration' – from the Muse or from the Holy Spirit – and it is these that I hope and believe will last. Few poets are remembered for more than a handful of poems and I would neither expect nor wish for myself that it should be otherwise.

Poems that I have no hesitation in omitting – mostly from the early volumes – are those written in a voice of insincere religiosity. Love-poems of a personal nature have also gone, as have those that in retrospect seem contrived, occasional poems of, for example, the last war. War, religion and personal love have all inspired great poetry, but only insofar as they have given wings to imagination. For myself they have impeded it.

To this day makers of anthologies tend to pick work from my early volumes, or often, as it seems, from other anthologies. For myself, poetry is only one aspect of the imaginative adventure of my life. My knowledge of the imaginative works of this and other countries, and above all my own detailed scholarly studies of William Blake, Thomas Taylor the Platonist and W. B. Yeats, some would consider as of more importance than my verse. These studies brought me to India, supreme civilisation of the Imagination, and indeed the country where I have felt 'Home at last!', not as poet or scholar but as a simple seeker for truth – as Yeats was though he never reached the shores of the Sub-continent. I could wish that my poetry might be read in the context of the whole scope of my life-work in the learning of the Imagination.

Believing as I do, with my Master, William Blake that 'One Power alone makes a poet – Imagination, The Divine Vision'; and with Yeats sharing his respect for the Vedic and Upanishadic tradition for which, as he saw them in Tagore, 'poetry and religion are the same thing', it is in the light of this perennial wisdom that I would wish my work to be judged. Better to be a little fish in the great ocean than to be a big fish in some literary rock-pool.

Kathleen Raine
20 June 2000

Contents

From *Stone and Flower* (1943)

From *Living in Time* (1946)

From *The Pythoness* (1949)

The Year One (1952)

The Hollow Hill (1965)

From *The Lost Country* (1971)

[XII]

From *The Oracle in the Heart* (1980)

From *The Presence* (1987)

From *Living With Mystery* (1992)

Uncollected and New Poems

Stone and Flower

(1943)

LYRIC

A BIRD sings on a matin tree
'Once such a bird was I.'

The sky's gaze says
'Remember your mother.'

Seas, trees and voices cry
'Nature is your nature.'

I reply
'I am what is not what it was.'
Seas, trees, and bird, alas!
Sea, tree, and bird was I.

'SEE, SEE CHRIST'S BLOOD STREAMS
IN THE FIRMAMENT'

THIS planetary blood
Streams crucifixion
In the space of bounded life's
Attraction and repulsion

Widening on the rude
Improvisation that the senses build
Staking extremities
To mark the victories

Whose
The streaming blood-bright
Iron-torrent of the wounds
    surpasses

As the cloudy mansions
Melt into clouds themselves
    extensions

[3]

Beyond the fought-on
Woman-wept victory-vaunted
dimensions.

INVOCATION

THERE is a poem on the way,
There is a poem all round me,
The poem is in the near future,
The poem is in the upper air
Above the foggy atmosphere
It hovers, a spirit
That I would make incarnate.
Let my body sweat
Let snakes torment my breast
My eyes be blind, ears deaf, hands distraught
Mouth parched, uterus cut out,
Belly slashed, back lashed,
Tongue slivered into thongs of leather
Rain stones inserted in my breasts,
Head severed,

If only the lips may speak,
If only the god will come.

PASSION

FULL of desire I lay, the sky wounding me,
Each cloud a ship without me sailing, each tree
Possessing what my soul lacked, tranquillity.

Waiting for the longed-for voice to speak
Through the mute telephone, my body grew weak
With the well-known and mortal death, heartbreak.

[4]

The language I knew best, my human speech
Forsook my fingers, and out of reach
Were Homer's ghosts, the savage conches of the beach.

Then the sky spoke to me in language clear,
Familiar as the heart, than love more near.
The sky said to my soul, 'You have what you desire.

'Know now that you are born along with these
Clouds, winds, and stars, and ever-moving seas
And forest dwellers. This your nature is.

Lift up your heart again without fear,
Sleep in the tomb, or breathe the living air,
This world you with the flower and with the tiger share.'

Then I saw every visible substance turn
Into immortal, every cell new born
Burned with the holy fire of passion.

This world I saw as on her judgment day
When the war ends, and the sky rolls away,
And all is light, love and eternity.

FAR-DARTING APOLLO

I SAW the sun step like a gentleman
Dressed in black and proud as sin.
I saw the sun walk across London
Like a young M.P. risen to the occasion.

His step was light, his tread was dancing,
His lips were smiling, his eyes glancing.
Over the Cenotaph in Whitehall
The sun took the wicket with my skull.

The sun plays tennis in the court of Geneva
With the guts of a Finn and the head of an Emperor,
The sun plays squash in a tomb of marble,
The horses of Apocalypse are in his stable.

The sun plays a game of darts in Spain,
Three by three in flight formation,
The invincible wheels of his yellow car
Are the discs that kindle the Chinese war.

The sun shows the world to the world,
Turns its own ghost on the terrified crowd,
Then plunges all images into the ocean
Of the nightly mass emotion.

Games of chance, and games of skill,
All his sports are games to kill.
I saw the murderer at evening lie
Bleeding on the deathbed sky.

His hyacinth breath, his laurel hair,
His blinding sight, his moving air,
My love, my grief, my weariness, my fears
Hid from me in a night of tears.

NOCTURN

For going out by night there is no place.
The sun upon the dark no region casts,
The rose beyond the evening cannot pass.

The flying sun withdraws colour and place,
Time, and all material attributes –
The rose beyond the angel cannot pass.

First of all flowers the crimson are in shade
With the unborn, the sleeping and the dead –
There is no place for going out by night.

And creatures all make room within the heart –
The heart no region and no sun requires,
Nor measuring time nor space for its desires.

The heart no region and no light requires,
The cannibal heart, that swallows up itself
Past the angelic sun, returns to life.

And errant night upon the table finds
That bread and wine upon the holy stone,
The body of the dead, and the unborn.

Since for going out by night there is no place
For the unborn, the sleeping, and the dead,
What sun, what sin, decrees the grail to fade?

THE RED LIGHT

THE women burn throughout the dead of night,
Their red signs through the curtained windows peep.
What sacrilegious hand puts out the light,
And for what fallen body do they weep?

Christ, as I die, I own it is for thee,
Love, human nature, origin and shame.
The same light in the shrine and brothel see,
Wherever human passion lights its flame.

For of that red star are we virgins all,
And the red heart is stilled by the red fire
That moves the spirit more than its desire
Towards unmoving love, the point of will.

HARVEST

Day is the hero's shield,
    Achilles' field,
The light days are the angels,
    We the seed.

Against eternal light and gorgon's face
    Day is the shield
    And we the grass
Native to fields of iron, and skies of brass.

TU NON SE' IN TERRA, SI COME TU CREDI

Not upon earth, as you suppose
Tower these rocks that turn the wind,
For on their summits angels stand.

Nor from the earth these waters rise –
To quench not thirst, but ecstasy
The waterfall leaps from the sky.

Those nameless clouds that storm and swirl
About the mountain are the veil
That from these sightless eyes shall fall

When senses faint into the ground,
And time and place go down the wind.

NIGHT IN MARTINDALE

Not in the rustle of water, the air's noise,
The roar of storm, the ominous birds, the cries –
The angel here speaks with a human voice.

Stone into man must grow, the human word
Carved by our whispers in the passing air

Is the authentic utterance of cloud,
The speech of flowing water, blowing wind,
Of silver moon and stunted juniper.

Words say, waters flow,
Rocks weather, ferns wither, winds blow, times go,
I write the sun's Love, and the stars' No.

THE HYACINTH

For James Madge

Time opens in a flower of bells
The mysteries of its hidden bed,
The altar of the ageless cells
Whose generations never have been dead.

So flower angels from the holy head,
So on the wand of darkness bright worlds hang.
Love laid the elements at the vital root,
Unhindered out of love these flowers spring.

The breath of life shapes darkness into leaves,
Each new born cell
Drinks from the star-filled well
The dark milk of the sky's peace.

The hyacinth springs on a dark star –
I see eternity give place to love.
It is the world unfolding into flower
The rose of life, the lily and the dove.

THE NIGHT-BLOWING CEREUS

WILDERNESS my thorny tree,
Midnight is my solitude,
Living in itself alone,
Love unfolds a poem to me.

Rising like a second moon
On the shadow falls the light,
Opening like a jessamine
For the moths that love the night.

Music for the ear of bats,
Silence for the wakeful heart,
Sounds that set the flame adance,
Dreams perceive as certainties,

And the spectral virgin moves
Into apotheosis,
Passionate in abstract trance
Thought becomes the bride of stars.

See her into distance pass
Beyond the doubting of the mind,
And beyond the heart's distress.

NOCTURN

NIGHT comes, an angel stands
Measuring out the time of stars,
Still are the winds, and still the hours.

It would be peace to lie
Still in the still hours at the angel's feet,
Upon a star hung in a starry sky,
But hearts another measure beat.

Each body, wingless as it lies,
Sends out its butterfly of night
With delicate wings and jewelled eyes.

And some upon day's shores are cast,
And some in darkness lost
In waves beyond the world, where float
Somewhere the islands of the blest.

IN TIME

THE beautiful rain falls, the unheeded angel
Lies in the street, spreadeagled under the footfall
That from the divine face wears away the smile

Whose tears run in the gutter, melting where
The stationary cars wait for departure;
The letter that says Ave is passed over,

For at the ever-present place the angel waits,
Passes through walls and hoardings, in dark porches
His face, wounded by us, for us and over us watches.

TO MY MOUNTAIN

SINCE I must love your north
Of darkness, cold, and pain,
The snow, the lonely glen,
Let me love true worth,

The strength of the hard rock,
The deafening stream of wind
That carries sense away
Swifter than flowing blood.

Heather is harsh to tears
And the rough moors
Give the buried face no peace
But make me rise,

And oh, the sweet scent, and purple skies!

AT THE WATERFALL

TOUCHING the mantle of the empty sky
With a clear sound on a canvas of silence,
The stream flows out of the clouds.

And on a rock, high on Place Fell
A gust of wind sounds
With a noise almost animal.

So much nearer than stillness they speak to me
I have heard too much silence,
Listened too long to the mute sky.

GOOD FRIDAY

THIS is the day, the cock has crowed
The passing of dreams, the death-cold dawn,
The setting of the star of Bethlehem
Behind a brow of stone.

This is the day the cock crowed in,
Crowed out the night; the lover straying
Beyond the body's grasp, now must return
Each entering his dimension like a tomb.

This is the hour of cock-crow and the men
Whose night was out of bounds, clock in again,
(as innocent in sleep as plant or stone)
Wake to do wrong, grow old, and suffer pain.

The cock crows out the night, and we remain
Outside eternity, the lover's dream
The soldier's sleep, the locked gates of the tomb,
Ghosts of our days, longing for night again.

ANGELUS

I SEE the blue, the green, the golden and the red,
I have forgotten all the angel said.

The flower, the leaf, the meadow and the tree,
But of the words I have no memory.

I hear the swift, the martin, and the wren,
But what was told me, past all thought is gone.

The dove, the rainbow, echo, and the wind,
But of the meaning, all is out of mind.

Only I know he spoke the word that sings its way
In my blood streaming, over rocks to sea,

A word engraved in the bone, that burns within
To apotheosis the substance of a dream,

That living I shall never hear again,
Because I pass, I pass, while dreams remain.

ENVOI

TAKE of me what is not my own,
My love, my beauty, and my poem –
The pain is mine, and mine alone.

See how against the weight in the bone
The hawk hangs perfect in mid-air –
The blood pays dear to raise it there,
The moment, not the bird, divine.

And see the peaceful trees extend
Their myriad leaves in leisured dance –
They bear the weight of sky and cloud
Upon the fountain of their veins.

In rose with petals soft as air
I bind for you the tides and fire –
The death that lives within the flower,
O gladly, love, for you I bear!

IN THE BECK

For Anna Madge

THERE is a fish, that quivers in the pool,
Itself a shadow, but its shadow, clear.
Catch it again and again, it still is there.

Against the flowing stream, its life keeps pace
With death – the impulse and the flash of grace
Hiding in its stillness, moves, to be motionless.

No net will hold it – always it will return
When the ripples settle, and the sand –
It lives unmoved, equated with the stream,
As flowers are fit for air, man for his dream.

A STRANGE EVENING

A LITTLE rain falls out of amethyst sky;
If there were a rainbow, it would be on the ground.
If I were here, that single swallow would be I,
If these green trees are heavy, their weight is in my hand.

If trees and fields are green, their veins run blood,
If there is a poem, it moves across the leaves.
If there is love, of trees and sky our bed.
Since there is such a sky, I cover it with peace,
With blue unbounded of the living eye,
The ox-eye pasture of the marguerite.

RETURNING AUTUMN

ALL creatures passionate for grace
Quest their desire through groves and seas
That flesh may win a human face,
And pain be crowned with holiness.

And lovers out of present days
Float back upon the body's dream
Of a green branch that dips and sways,
Caught in the current of a stream.

ON LEAVING ULLSWATER

1

THE air is full of a farewell –
Deserted by the silver lake
Lies the wild world, overturned.
Cities rise where mountains fell,
The furnace where the phoenix burned.

The lake is in my dream,
The tree is in my blood,
The past is in my bones,
The flowers of the wood
I love with long past loves.
I fear with many deaths
The presence of the night,
And in my memory read
The scripture of the leaves –
    Only myself how strange
    To the strange present come!

LEAVING MARTINDALE

    SHALL I be true
    As these hills bind me
    As these skies find me,
    As waters weather me,
    As leaves crown me?
    My kiss keep faith
    With death and birth,
    My joy with pain,
    My heaven with earth?

    I love you as the air
    Enfolds the earth,
    As darkness holds a star,
    As waters, life.
    You are the smiling heart,
    The sunlit noon
    Of one who soon must sleep
    Her death alone.

Shall I be true?
Love binds in vain
Whom death must loose –
The flesh, the pain
That knows you now
Soon will not know
That love must pass,
That times must go.

LONDON REVISITED

HAUNTING these shattered walls, hung with our past
That no electron and no sun can pierce,
We visit rooms in dreams
Where we ourselves are ghosts.

There is no foothold for our solid world,
No hanging Babylon for the certain mind
In rooms tattered by wind, wept on by rain.

Wild as the tomb, wild as the mountainside
A storm of hours has shaken the finespun world
Tearing away our palaces, our faces, and our days.

THE WIND OF TIME

TIME blows a tempest – how the days run high,
Deep graves are open between hour and hour,
A current sweeps the streets and houses by
Too fast to board them. Cities are wrecked by night
And we left drowning in this empty dawn.
No land is seaworthy, no bird in sight.

And on the shores, after the tempest lie
Fragments of past delight, and of past selves,
Dead rooms and houses, with the stranded shells.

THE GOLDEN LEAF

THE floating of a leaf that fell
A wounded star upon the tide
Out of the world, free in farewell,

I saw – not able to withhold
The vanishing moment with my sight
From the lock of living heart,

And down the rapid nerves, the light
Plunged, where the thundering stream of blood
Engulfs each mote within the eye,

Upon the dark pool of my thought
Turned slowly, sinking into past,
Then poised on a reflected sky.

HAPPY THE CAPTIVE
AND ENCHANTED SOULS . . .

HAPPY the captive and enchanted souls
Seduced by love to stay, with eyes like flowers
That weave their hanging gardens in the sun!
(O birth that wakes in me, as each day rises,
And death that takes me as each moment passes,
Bud opening, and leaf falling) Incarnation
Moves with divine trespass into the dawn
Earth's seamless dress, eternally made man.

VEGETATION

O NEVER harm the dreaming world,
The world of green, the world of leaves,
But let its million palms unfold
The adoration of the trees.

It is a love in darkness wrought
Obedient to the unseen sun,
Longer than memory, a thought
Deeper than the graves of time.

The turning spindles of the cells
Weave a slow forest over space,
The dance of love, creation,
Out of time moves not a leaf,
And out of summer, not a shade.

SEED

FROM star to star, from sun and spring and leaf,
And almost audible flowers whose sound is silence,
And in the common meadows, springs the seed of life.

Now the lilies open, and the rose
Released by summer from the harmless graves
That, centuries deep, are in the air we breathe,
And in our earth, and in our daily bread.

External and innate dimensions hold
The living forms, but not the force of life;
For that interior and holy tree
That in the heart of hearts outlives the world
Spreads earthly shade into eternity.

THE SILVER STAG

My silver stag is fallen – on the grass
Under the birch-trees he lies, my king of the woods,
That I followed on the mountain, over the swift streams,
He is gone under the leaves, under the past.

On the horizon of the dawn he stood,
The target of my eager sight; that shone
Oh from the sun, or from my kindled heart –
Outlined in sky, shaped on the infinite.

What, so desiring, was my will with him,
What wished-for union of blood or thought
In single passion held us, hunter and victim?
Already gone, when into the branched woods I pursued him.

Mine he is now, my desired, my awaited, my beloved,
Quiet he lies, as I touch the contours of his proud head,
Mine, this horror, this carrion of the wood,
Already melting underground, into the air, out of the world.

Oh, the stillness, the peace about me
As the garden lives on, the flowers bloom,
The fine grass shimmers, the flies burn,
And the stream, the silver stream, runs by.

Lying for the last time down on the green ground
In farewell gesture of self-love, softly he curved
To rest the delicate foot that is in my hand,
Empty as a moth's discarded crysalis.

My bright yet blind desire, your end was this
Death, and my winged heart murderous
Is the world's broken heart, buried in his,
Between whose antlers starts the crucifix.

THE SPEECH OF BIRDS

For Helen Sutherland

IT is not birds that speak, but men learn silence;
They know and need no language; leaf-wise
In shadowy flight, threading the leafy trees,
Expressive only of the world's long thoughts,
Absolute rises their one-pointed song,
Not from a heart divided, and in pain.

The sweet-eyed, unregarding beasts
Waking and sleeping wear the natural grace.
The innocent order of the stars and tides
An impulse in the blood-stream circulates.
Obedient to one living pulse,
With them, at heart, converse the saints.

We, ignorant and outcast, stand
Wondering at the swallow's flight
Gazing at the open hand,
Questioning the lines of fate –
Each individual destiny
Preying on an exiled mind.

Our words, our concepts, only name
A world of shadows; for the truth is plain
That visited Jacob in a dream,
And Moses, from the burning desert heard,
Or angels in annunciation bring.

LONDON TREES

OUT of the roads of London springs the forest,
Over and underworld, the veritable Eden
Here we have planted for our solitude,
Those planes, where thoughts unblamed among the leaves may run.

Sensing us, the trees tremble in their sleep,
The living leaves recoil before our fires,
Baring to us war-charred and broken branches,
And seeing theirs, we for our own destruction weep.

And women, sore at heart, trying to pray
Unravel the young buds with anxious fingers
Searching for God, who has gone far away,
Yet still at evening in the green world lingers.

Obedient still the toiling trees
Lift up their fountains, where still waters rise
Upwards into life, filled from the surrounding skies
To quench the sorrows thirsting in the world's eyes.

THE SPHERE

O THE happy ending, the happy ending
That the fugue promised, that love believed in,
That perfect star, that bright transfiguration,

Where has it vanished, now that the music is over,
The certainty of being, the heart in flower,
Ourselves, perfect at last, affirmed as what we are?

The world, the changing world stands still while lovers kiss,
And then moves on – what was our fugitive bliss,
The dancer's ecstasy, the vision, and the rose?

There is no end, no ending – steps of a dance, petals of flowers
Phrases of music, rays of the sun, the hours
Succeed each other, and the perfect sphere
Turns in our hearts the past and future, near and far,
Our single soul, atom, and universe.

NEW YEAR 1943

STAIRWAYS into space, and windows into sky,
And the tear-wet streets, with cloud-torn moonlight shining,
Ways underground are open, and the trains are running
Oh to what end, in this dream-entangled city?

The streets were full tonight
With the dense human darkness – noisier
With the talking of feet, and laughter,
Night-cries of 'taxi,' and the flagging light

Of men and women walking in their thought
Like ghosts in overcoats and uniforms,
Their bodies, grown invisible, scarcely felt,
Alone, or mated, in the London night.

You meet them everywhere – their touching hands,
Fingers made intricate with bones and nerves,
Playing like birds; or resting, still in sleep
Though eyes are open, while men's thoughts run deep.

Oh where, into the night, into the underground,
Into the sky, into dark seas, do they go,
The young boys who flash torches in the dark,
For their sweethearts in mimic dress, the counterpart
Of war, the service-girl, the glamour-girl, the tart?

Girls' hair, like florists' flowers, their coloured lips and eyes
In farewell greet the R.A.F.'s young heroes,
Gauche in the close-up of love, and close-up death,
Never in meagre childhood taught how to die, or kiss.

They stray, enchanted, in this crumbling city,
Where the safe homes of childhood house the winds,
Through whose uncertain present, lies our way
To love, to death – our certainty, our strangeness.

THE HEALING SPRING

PATIENTLY the earth's wounds close.
The womb heals of its sons
As bark over a torn branch grows.

That we were ever one, my blood
Obedient to the spring, forgets,
And growth obliterates the past
That lies within my heart like death.

Oh Love forgive the happiness
That overgrows and seals my grief.

THE MESSENGERS

Two angels came quietly
Into my room
In the ordinary day

With the common dust
That floats on the light
Of any sunbeam.

They were not near, nor far,
Nor long in sight,
With words wonderful to hear,
But hard to remember.

Carrying their love I came
To you in the evening,
To give all, to take nothing.

But when you kissed me, in my joy
I forgot the night and day,
And what the angels sent by me.

They came again long after
While it was not too late,
And told me to remember.

You came in anger, and at night
And in my grief and pain
The words of love I could not find.

THE HANDS

As I was most alone
With troubled thoughts,
A pair of hands held mine
Like folded leaves,
Closed over me
The palms on which are traced
The veins of history.

Held me – as between father and mother
A child lies
Healed me – as between lover and lover
There is peace
Ruled me – as they rule the suns and stars
And saintly journeys.

Held between sorrow and joy, between dark and light,
My hand passes
Across the hours, across the fields, across the pages
Of day and night
And like the Northumbrian boy who could not write,
I'll learn my letters from the angels.
For the words in my heart.

HEROES

THIS war's dead heroes, who has seen them?
They rise in smoke above the burning city,
Faint clouds, dissolving into sky.

And who sifting the Libyan sand can find
The tracery of a human hand,
The faint impression of an absent mind,
The fade-out of a soldier's day dream?

You'll know your love no more, nor his sweet kisses –
He's forgotten you, girl, and in the idle sun
In long green grass that the east wind caresses
The seed of man is ravished by the corn.

FROM
Living in Time
(1946)

SEEN IN A GLASS

THE Venus in my mirror sighs
  As one who suffers life in vain.
I see in non-existent eyes
The incommunicable selfish pain.

Such feelings move those images
And dreams that living creatures are,
As are inherent in our frames
Of mutable earth, air and fire.

Unwise we feel, but wise we know
Living in time is but to seem –
Like green leaves on a tree we grow,
But each must fall and fade alone.

WINTER SOLSTICE

EVERYWHERE
The first bird of the year
Has sung a valentine
Tuned to the last winter star.

In cold shrill voice,
The first loves of spring,
Leafless as the blooming
Of jasmine trees.

The star's intervals
Lead in the first winds,
Open the first buds,
Hold the first pauses

That wait for hope,
Expectant of music,
Foreknowing leaves unfold,
Faithful to heart's beat.

The green winter stars
Of thistle and scabious
Open in slow cadence
Of the tall sweet flower,

The first light of dawn
On the heart's desolate stone
Will reveal a mountain
In a blue sky shining,

Each star is answering
Another, and the sun,
That bridegroom, kind once again,
Northward to me returning.

THE TREES IN TUBS

LITTLE laurel trees, your roots can find
No mountain, yet your leaves extend
Beyond your own world, into mine
Perennial wands, unfolding in my thought
The budding evergreen of time.

MOURNING IN SPRING 1943

O YOU girls, girl friends, you who have also loved
The fertile god Osiris, and Adonis
Whose garden has flowered for centuries from our blood,
Though love was different for each of us,
Know now, he is dying, our lover, dying all over the world.

Dying all over the world – his death will stain
The green fields crimson, extinguish the bright south,
Make the north frigid for ever, embitter the ocean,
From the east to the west, his funeral blackens the sun's path.

These were our men, whose destiny is the desert,
And those who were last seen struggling in the sea,
Though not for long – the waves now have washed them away
And their ears and mouths and hearts are muted with sand.

These were our men – now nameless among death's millions,
Our sons, our darlings that we have cherished from the world's
        creation,
These were the lovers that wiped all tears from our eyes,
And now our sterile wombs and broken hearts
Are the measure of war's disaster, and love's price.

FOR POSTERITY

On a drawing of Patterdale in 1830

ALL life, tumbled together in a storm
And the crags stand out clear in the lightning.
The wind, like a bolting horse, pounds down the valley,
The sheep, like vegetation, draw to earth,
And trees, like animate things, tear at their roots and groan.

That was in 1830. That storm long since was over.
So, my tempestuous love, closed in a quiet book,
And in a quiet grave, disturbs no heart but yours,
Reader, stretched on the summer grass
Waiting for tea-time, and shadows growing longer.

PRAYER

THE laws of blind unrest, not art,
Have built this room in time and space,
The furniture of human sense
That bounds my sorrow, curbs delight.

But to the grail, these fragile walls
Are thinner than a floating dream,
And here the heart's full measure fills
With what is worldwide, yet within.

And gathering round me those I know
In the close circle of a prayer,
The sleepers, the forgetful, grow
In love, though not in presence, near.

My distant ones, this heart on fire
Is for a candle in your night,
While you lie safe within that care
Whose dark is sleep, whose waking, light.

THE TREE OF HEAVEN

THE peace of flowers. Heaven like a tree grows
In silence; has no voice
Till they come and perch in the branches, images of words
From two worlds, birds and angels,
Inhabitants of mute leaves, lovers of the plant's rapt blindness.

Heaven, simple like a seed, from its minute beginning
Rooted in flesh and blood, instinct with death and pain
Grows complex, manifold; grows great with living,
With green and blossom and bough, sky-covering
With world, where nothing was, until heaven's spring.

Pattern of tree and man, unfold within me –
Branch where the veins run, quicken at the heart,
Be felt in every nerve, and fruitful at the breast,
Vine, pattern of Christ, interior quiet,
Quicken this barrenness, flower in my desert!

FOUR POEMS OF MARY MAGDALENE

1

REMEMBER Mary Magdalene,
Once in a night so near you and so far.
Held by her beauty and her golden hair
Embraced and yet most desolate you were.

Those tresses could not bind you – you were falling
For ever out of her white arms like a waterfall.
The senses' frail net cast in eternity
Meshes where suns, birds, worlds and lovers flow away.

She mourned for earthly love, but could not save
The creature from its loneliness,
Or hold a lover back one hour from death.

And her nameless love consumed
With grief beside you all that night,
The hidden vigil of the heart,
The soul's unquenchable desire for God.

2

INTO the night the Magdalene turned away
Into a sleep more wide than waking
Passed through the evening doors of the outgoing day.

Love drew her on towards her tryst with God;
Guided like a night moth to its chalice,
She entered the soul's darkness like a garden.

Earth's visible flowers from every sense withdrawn,
What jasmine, what nocturnal primrose, bloom
By light invisible of the heavenly sun?

Secret and evergreen garden, living water,
You were there from the beginning, and the rose
Unfolding at heart for ever into quietness,

And she, daughter of Eve, not whom she sought
A world of grief away until she found Him
Her love, her Lord, already before her in the garden.

3

CHILD of the town, she knew the faces of people
As country girls know all the kinds of flowers.
She knew in men the cruel, the timid and the generous,
The commonplace, the bestial and the beautiful.

And sometimes in the proud bearing of a man,
The fineness of the hair, the eyes' deep gaze,
A voice, a mouth's delicate line, a hand's gentleness
She fancied she had found the perfect one.

But learned how all are mortal, and forebore.
Practised how to give all and to take nothing,
Learned not to look too deep, or draw too near,
To bear inviolate her loneliness;
Her art, to be withdrawn and like the earth,
A cloud, the sea, a song, a garden or a river.

Was it His face she knew or was God known to her
In healing a beggar of a lifetime's sin and blindness,
Or taking up a child into His arms,
Or with a scourge striding in Heaven's anger through
    the temple?
Or was it enough only to hear His voice to know Him?

Easy for her to see God in man!
She knew the weak who ask for love – He gave.
The proud who scorn the woman – He received her.

[34]

She had endured the lust of men – but He had none.
And yet she knew herself beloved by Him alone
Whom, weeping, she asked only to adore.

4

THEY see her now as pure transparency.
The stained-glass window of her face
Where the light pours all day
Is framed upon two worlds – one is ours
And one the outer and invisible sky.

Her heart has never stirred out of that joy
Wherein she saw God sitting in her house.
When the sun shines on her, she seems to smile.

His radiance flows through her over us,
Down her waved golden hair like water falls.

THE SPRING

Song

OUT of hope's eternal spring
Bubbled once my mountain stream
Moss and sundew, fern and fell,
Valley, summer, tree and sun
All rose up, and all are gone.

By the spring I saw my love
(All who have parted once must meet,
First we live, and last forget),
With the stars about his head
With the future in his heart
Lay the green earth at my feet.

Now by the spring I stand alone
Still are its singing waters flowing;
Oh never thought I here to greet
Shadowy death who comes this way
Where hope's waters rise and play!

THE MOMENT

To write down all I contain at this moment
I would pour the desert through an hour-glass,
The sea through a water-clock,
Grain by grain and drop by drop
Let in the trackless, measureless, mutable seas and sands.

For earth's days and nights are breaking over me
The tides and sands are running through me,
And I have only two hands and a heart to hold the desert and
    the sea.

What can I contain of it? It escapes and eludes me
The tides wash me away
The desert shifts under my feet.

INFINITE

Like the sea-sounding blood that children hear
At night when the ear's shell is held to sleep,
Infinity flows round us with the dark,
And heaven hangs behind the window-curtain.

The infinite recedes beyond the farthest star
And here, no less remote, though I can gather it
(A hair's breadth of it is as wide as night),
Astral upon the grass in manifold it flowers.

It is the star whose light the eye takes in like love,
The flower that opens its star in the mind's eye
It is the eye within whose iris the star flowers.

It is that seed grown pregnant in the mind
Sprung from an earth alien as any star
That makes of thought a tree profound as night,
That makes the human scope the orbit of all suns

Where love the infinite eternal rose
Fills with its implicated whorls
The hierarchies of being with its petals.

THE GODDESS

SHE goes by many names; Diana of the sacred wood
With manifold breasts like acorns on an oak
And primitive features, image of the joy men take
In her, all powerful where in caves and shadows lie
Those mortal beasts, her offspring and her prey.

We have known her as archaic mother Eve.
The earth is all her cradle
Where we awake from our first sleep to see
Her flower-face bending over us
The sky, the rowan, and the elder-tree.

Some worship her as queen of angels, Venus of the sea,
House of gold, palace of ivory,
Gate of heaven and rose of mystery,
Inviolate and ever-virgin earth,
Daughter of time and mother of eternity.

Lover, in your true love's body lies
The sacred darkness of Diana's grove,
Hers are the careful arms that Adam's children hold,
And in her heart the cause of joy, the house of gold,
The gate of Heaven, the ever-virgin rose.

THE ROSE

WHAT does the eye see?
A rose-bud on a paradise tree.

What does hope say?
A rose shall fill time with eternity!

What is memory's refrain?
'I was that rose before the world began.'

What does thought foretell?
Petal upon petal,
World within world, star within cell.

What sings love then?
'I am the rose, that crimson rose is mine.'

Why comes death this way?
To take away, to take my rose away.

What lies in the immortal centre hidden?
Mary on the golden throne of Heaven.

And in the heart of Heaven what lives, what grows?
The heart of Heaven is the rose, the rose!

FROM
The Pythoness
(1949)

AIR

ELEMENT that utters doves, angels and cleft flames,
The bees of Helicon and the cloudy houses,
Impulse of music and the word's equipoise,

Dancer that never wearies of the dance
That prints in the blown dust eternal wisdom
Or carves its abstract sculptures in the snow,
The wind unhindered passes beyond its trace.

But from a high fell on a summer day
Sometimes below you may see the air like water,
The dazzle of the light upon its waves
That flow unbroken to the end of the world.

The bird of god descends between two moments
Like silence into music, opening a way through time.

WATER

THE water-Venus in dissolving beauty
Pours into our night-cities her seas' multitude,
Steeps with her dew the gardens of the earth,
And in our veins, still tidal to her moon
The life-blood surges out to her in waves
That break in tears or fleeting vain delight.

But in mid-ocean of desire
The King of Fishes stands
Upon the teeming seas, and to him rise
Like salmon to the poacher's light
Miraculous drafts of Venus' spawn
As from her element we are drawn,
From living waters into birth.

FIRE

ALL begins in fire and ends in fire.
The fountains and cool springs return to flame
And at the sun's approaching wheel, the dew
Ascends the rainbow circle into the sole white.

All that begins in darkness kindles
Into the burning of desire
And from desire into sight,
Seer and seen consuming in one light
When rocks melt in the sun, and mountains pour
Into those flames that to the bound are hell
But to the freed elements, pure delight.

Our forms are fearful of the fires that burn away
Self and identify, but in the dark of the heart
The candle of the soul still for the bridegroom burns,
And in the hidden electron of the water
Consumes the zeal of burning for the last day.

LENTEN FLOWERS

PRIMROSE, anemone, bluebell, moss
Grow in the kingdom of the cross

And the ash-tree's purple bud
Dresses the spear that sheds his blood.

With the thorns that pierce his brow
Soft encircling petals grow

For in each flower the secret lies
Of the tree that crucifies.

Garden by the water clear
All must die that enter here!

STORM

God in me is the fury on the bare heath
God in me shakes the interior kingdom of my heaven.
God in me is the fire wherein I burn.

God in me swirling cloud and driving rain
God in me cries a lonely nameless bird
God in me beats my head upon a stone.

God in me the four elements of storm
Raging in the shelterless landscape of the mind
Outside the barred doors of my Goneril heart.

ABSOLUTION

Sometimes by angels of the mind
The absolving words are said,
Sometimes the heart is touched with mercy in a dream.

Lost innocent flower faces smiling
Into childhood's tear-wet eyes
Bless with divine forgiveness from the grass.

Birds sing their phrases from green places,
Pure voice that self-imprisoned lovers hear
Clear above the clamorous mourning of desire.

The deafening thunder of the passionate tide
In the dark heart that rages against its shore
Batters the senses with the absolution
Of the blood-beat of life's continuance.

Chairs, withering flowers, mirror and clock and hearth,
Mute things of home that anger has assailed
Outraged and sorrowful proffer their silent pardon.

Flower of the violated grass, voice of the lost grove,
Unheard, unheeded eloquence of wronged things,
Thunder that rends the self-accusing soul,
Voice of those bleeding silent wounds ourselves have given
Sole divine judgment on the murderous heart,
Forgiveness, too terrible to be born!

MANDALA

The centre of the mandala is everywhere,
Wherever the eye falls
The mystery begins to unfold; it is there,
The growing-point of love, an ever-opening rose
Perceived as light on leaf or shadow under,
And in the brooding heart the wings stir
Of the bird whose flight is through a thousand skies.

The centre of the mandala is the secret
We have always known:
Sometimes a hazel-nut in the palm of the hand,
Sometimes it covers the whole sky,
Or rains down on a city
Making strange places all familiar
Because the light that touches them is our own.

The centre of the mandala is possibility
Of incarnation, seed of the tree
About whose beams the myriad stars turn,
I the infinity where all selves converge
Into the perennial circle of the sun.

WORD MADE FLESH

WORD whose breath is the world-circling atmosphere,
Word that utters the world that turns the wind,
Word that articulates the bird that speeds upon the air,

Word that blazes out the trumpet of the sun,
Whose silence is the violin-music of the stars,
Whose melody is the dawn, and harmony the night,

Word traced in water of lakes, and light on water,
Light on still water, moving water, waterfall
And water colours of cloud, of dew, of spectral rain,

Word inscribed on stone, mountain range upon range of stone,
Word that is fire of the sun and fire within
Order of atoms, crystalline symmetry,

Grammar of five-fold rose and six-fold lily,
Spiral of leaves on a bough, helix of shells,
Rotation of twining plants on axes of darkness and light,

Instinctive wisdom of fish and lion and ram,
Rhythm of generation in flagellate and fern,
Flash of fin, beat of wing, heartbeat, beat of the dance,

Hieroglyph in whose exact precision is defined
Feather and insect-wing, refraction of multiple eyes,
Eyes of the creatures, oh myriadfold vision of the world,

Statement of mystery, how shall we name
A spirit clothed in world, a world made man?

WINTER FIRE

THE presence of nature in my winter room
With curtains drawn across the clouds and stars,
Lakes, fells, and green sweet meadows far away
Is fire, older and more wild than they.

Fire will outlast them all and take them all
For into fire the autumn woods must fall.
Spring blossoming is the slow combustion of the tree,
The phoenix fire that burns bird, beast and flower away.

Once Troy and Dido's Carthaginian pyre
And Baldur's ship, and fabulous London burning,
Robes, wooden walls and crystal palaces
In the apotheosis were such flames as these

Flames more fluent than water of a mountain stream,
Flames more delicate and swift than air,
Flames more impassable than walls of stone,
Destructive and irrevocable as time.

Essential fire is the unhindered spirit
That, laid upon the lips of prophecy
Frees all the shining elements of the soul;
Whose burning teaches love the way to die
And selves to undergo their ultimate destruction
Upon those flaming ramparts of the world
That rise between our fate, and the lost garden.

FORMULATION

Into which of the mind's moulds
Will vision flow,
The divine formulation grow?

Once a woman perceived a holy head
Dropping its shining blood
Like fish-scales, or like rain-drops from the eaves.

Elsewhere it is a lotus-flower
Opening from the self-encentred Buddha
Composed for ever like a still dancer,

And once in Lambeth a hidden grain of sand
Held all the world that vision can command,
The great eternity within a poet's mind.

Grandiose archaic faces,
Contours of former souls' experience
Stand between my vision and what they saw,

Therefore come as a bird within the mind,
Or as a single leaf upon a tree of leaves
Suddenly made shining by the sun,

Or break like day upon a simple stone
Or in a dazzle of sunlight upon water,
Come as a jewelled moth, a budding flower

Come in a form I shall not too much fear.

ISIS WANDERER

THIS too is an experience of the soul
The dismembered world that once was the whole god
Whose broken fragments now lie dead.
This passing of reality itself is real.

Gathering under my black cloak the remnants of life
That lie dishonoured among people and places
I search the twofold desert of my solitude,
The outward perished world, and the barren mind.

Once he was present, numinous, in the house of the world,
Wearing day like a garment, his beauty manifest
In corn and man as he journeyed down the fertile river.
With love he filled my distances of night.

I trace the contour of his hand fading upon a cloud,
And this his blood flows from a dying soldier's wound.
In broken fields his body is scattered and his limbs lie
Spreadeagled like wrecked fuselage in the sand.

His skull is a dead cathedral, and his crown's rays
Glitter from worthless tins and broken glass.
His blue eyes are reflected from pools in the gutter,
And his strength is the desolate stone of fallen cities.

Oh in the kitchen-midden of my dreams
Turning over the potsherds of past days
Shall I uncover his loved desecrated face?
Are the unfathomed depths of sleep his grave?

Beyond the looming dangerous end of night
Beneath the vaults of fear do his bones lie,
And does the maze of nightmare lead to the power within?
Do menacing nether waters cover the fish king?

I place the divine fragments into the mandala
Whose centre is the lost creative power,
The sun, the heart of God, the lotus, the electron
That pulses world upon world, ray upon ray
That he who lived on the first may rise on the last day.

DUST

ONLY my dust is never laid
And only I must always die.
This dust has travelled with the earth since suns were made
Yet never left eternity

Whose rule is traced upon my hand that writes,
That bears the seal of nature's forms and states;
The stars obey that order, and the grass,
The beautiful, the innocent, and the saints.

These bones have known the molten rocks outpoured
In transmutation of the solar fires,
Obedient to the laws that I have broken,
The power and glory of the reigning sun.

My blood streams with the motion of the tides,
The fall of rain and cataract, storm and calm,
Has undergone the freezing of the ice
And the baroque assumption of the clouds.

The shape of the cross is laid upon the void
By the first flash that leaps between the poles.
The world is built upon a separation
Whose distance the long light-years cannot close.
The wound proliferates, the rift extends.

Man's passion is predestined in the tree,
The cross-beams of the heavens, vegetation,
The thorns, the iron, and the organic thirst
From the beginning raise his calvary.

The dust sweeps through the figures of a dance,
Moves in its ritual transit like a bride
Imprinting shells and flowers with spiral forms that pass
To fossil wastes and whirling nebulae,
Weaving the rose, the lamb, and the world's darling child,
And then unmakes again the world the dance has made.

EX NIHILO

Out of nothing we are made,
Our cities rise upon the void,

And in chromium-plated bars,
Shadows drink their fill of tears,

Women's transient fingers pass
Over silks and flowers and glass,

Cameras and motor-cars
Spin on the hub of nothingness
On which revolve the years and stars.

Beyond the houses and the fields
Rise the forest-shrouded hills,

[49]

And upon each leaf is traced
The pattern of the eternal mind
That summons kingdoms from the dust.

Above the forests lie the clouds,
White fields where the soaring sight
Rests on the air's circumference,

And distant constellations move
About the centre of a thought
By the fiat of that love

Whose being is the breath of life,
The terra firma that we tread,
The divine body that we eat,
The incarnation that we live.

THE TRANSIT OF THE GODS

STRANGE that the self's continuum should outlast
The Virgin, Aphrodite, and the Mourning Mother,
All loves and griefs, successive deities
That hold their kingdom in the human breast.

Abandoned by the gods, woman with an ageing body
That half remembers the Annunciation,
The passion and the travail and the grief
That wore the mask of my humanity,

I marvel at the soul's indifference.
For in her theatre the play is done,
The tears are shed; the actors, the immortals
In their ceaseless manifestation, elsewhere gone,

And I who have been virgin and Aphrodite,
The mourning Isis and the queen of corn
Wait for the last mummer, dread Persephone
To dance my dust at last into the tomb.

ENCOUNTER

FALLEN to what strange places
Love travels pilgrim,
And into what deep dream
Descend these bottomless synthetic stairs?

Out of the void, impassable locked doors,
Clocks, telephones and sound-proof rooms
Proliferate like cancer in the mind
Interior prisons vaster than the dark.

There I the dreamer stood
Watching the handsome soldiers pass
In uniform of time, conscripts of place
Coming and going in the mind of God.

And there I met my love
Whom I had known before the stars were made;
We paused in recognition, and I said,
'Carry this memory, an amulet against death'.

But he replied,
'This is death's house, where love must learn to die.'
And time moved on again, and we were parted.

OUT OF NOTHING

WITHIN the centre of the rose
Seed out of the silence grows

Its crimson heart the night enfolds
The atom's void, the source of worlds

From whose unfathomed chaos rise
Star and leviathan from interior skies.

Here build a house where love may come
From the ends of darkness home,

Here the virgin waits alone
For her lover, for her son,

Here the mother wraps her child
In warm dress of flesh and blood

Pitying love's nakedness,
Love, the child of the abyss.

LYRIC

Low laughter of light
In gleaming sky
Dawns over deeps
Of memory.

If I could listen
I should hear,
If I could look,
I should see
The moving waves
Of soundless sea.

But eyes blind me,
Thoughts bind me,
Time ties me,
I turn away.

It was I who laughed
And I was the day,
The tremor of joy
And the arch of light
That spans the sky.

SELF

WHO am I, who
Speaks from the dust,
Who looks from the clay?

Who hears
For the mute stone,
For fragile water feels
With finger and bone?

Who for the forest breathes the evening,
Sees for the rose,
Who knows
What the bird sings?

Who am I, who for the sun fears
The demon dark,
In order holds
Atom and chaos?

Who out of nothingness has gazed
On the beloved face?

QUESTION AND ANSWER

THAT which is being the only answer
The question is its measure. Ask the flower
And the answer unfolds in eloquent petals about the centre;
Ask fire, and the rose bursts into flame and terror.

Ask water and the streams flow and dew falls;
Shell's minute spiral wisdom forms in pools.
Earth answers fields and gardens and the grave; birds rise
Into the singing air that opens boundless skies.

Womb knows the eternal union and its child,
Heart the blood-sacrifice of the wounded god.
Death charts the terrible negative infinity,
And with the sun rises perpetual day.

THE CLUE

ONLY the virgin knows the life story,
The myth implicit in the silk-spun bud
Whose leaves are the unopened pages of the heart.

The gossamer of her dream floats out across the night;
Its fragile thread upholds the somnambulist –
(Let none awaken my beloved, or she is lost)

When the angel came, she knew his face
And to the stranger asking a strange thing
Gave the answer predestined before time.

Young spiders weave at first their perfect webs,
Later, less certain, they weave worse.
Old age spins tattered cobwebs, rags and shreds.

Mater Dolorosa, at the end of a spent myth,
Remembering the past, but not the future,
Has lost her clue, like an old spider,

For time undoes us, darkness defaces
The figures of Penelope's night loom.
Revolving stars wind up the tenuous threads of day-dream
And the old spinner ravels skeins of death.

WOMAN TO LOVER

I AM fire
Stilled to water,

A wave
Lifting from the abyss.

In my veins
The moon-drawn tide rises
Into a tree of flowers
Scattered in sea-foam.

I am air
Caught in a net,

The prophetic bird
That sings in a reflected sky,

I am a dream before nothingness,
I am a crown of stars,
I am the way to die.

THE JOURNEY

For Winifred Nicholson

As I went over fossil hill
I gathered up small jointed stones,
And I remembered the archaic sea
Where once these pebbles were my bones.

As I walked on the Roman wall
The wind blew southward from the pole.
Oh I have been that violence hurled
Against the ramparts of the world.

At nightfall in an empty kirk
I felt the fear of all my deaths:
Shapes I had seen with animal eyes
Crowded the dark with mysteries.

I stood beside a tumbling beck
Where thistles grew upon a mound
That many a day had been my home,
Where now my heart rots in the ground.

I was the trout that haunts the pool,
The shadowy presence of the stream.
Of many many lives I leave
The scattered bone and broken wing.

I was the dying animal
Whose cold eye closes on a jagged thorn,
Whose carcass soon is choked with moss,
Whose skull is hidden by the fern.

My footprints sink in shifting sand
And barley-fields have drunk my blood,
My wisdom traced the spiral of a shell,
My labour raised a cairn upon a fell.

Far I have come and far must go,
In many a grave my sorrow lies,
But always from dead fingers grow
Flowers that I bless with living eyes.

THE TRAVELLER

A HUNDRED years I slept beneath a thorn
Until the tree was root and branches of my thought,
Until white petals blossomed in my crown.

A thousand years I floated in a lake
Until my brimful eye could hold
The scattered moonlight and the burning cloud.

Mine is the gaze that knows
Eyebright, asphodel, and briar rose.
I have seen the rainbow open, the sun close.

A wind that blows about the land
I have raised temples of snow, castles of sand
And left them empty as a dead hand.

A winged ephemerid I am born
With myriad eyes and glittering wings
That flames must wither or waters drown.

I must live, I must die,
I am the memory of all desire,
I am the world's ashes, and the kindling fire.

THE WORLD

It burns in the void
Nothing upholds it
Still it travels.

Travelling the void
Upheld by burning
Nothing is still.

Burning it travels
The void upholds it
Still it is nothing.

Nothing it travels
A burning void
Upheld by stillness.

PEACE OF MIND

If the pool were still
The reflected world
Of tottering houses,
The falling cities,
The quaking mountains
Would cohere on the surface

And stars invisible
To the troubled mind
Be seen in water
Drawn from the soul's
Bottomless well.

THE END OF LOVE

Now he is dead
How should I know
My true love's arms
From wind and snow?

No man I meet
In field or house,
Though in the street
A hundred pass.

The hurrying dust
Has never a face,
No longer human
In man or woman.

Now he is gone
Why should I mourn
My true love more
Than mud or stone?

The Year One

(1952)

NORTHUMBRIAN SEQUENCE

So seems the life of man, O King, as a sparrow's flight
through the hall when you are sitting at meat in winter-tide,
the fire on the hearth, the icy rainstorm without.
    The sparrow flies in at one door and tarries for a moment
in the light and heat of the hearth-fire, then flies forth into
the darkness whence it came.
    *Words attributed to an ealdorman, in Bede's account of the
conversion of Eadwine, King of Northumberland.*

1

Pure I was before the world began,
        I was the violence of wind and wave,
I was the bird before bird ever sang.

I was never still,
I turned upon the axis of my joy,
I was the lonely dancer on the hill,

The rain upon the mountainside,
The rising mist,
I was the sea's unrest.

I wove the web of colour
Before the rainbow,
The intricacy of the flower
Before the leaf grew.

I was the buried ore,
The fossil forest,
I knew the roots of things:
Before death's kingdom
I passed through the grave.

Times out of mind my journey
Circles the universe
And I remain
Before the first day.

Him I praise with my mute mouth of night
Uttering silences until the stars
Hang at the still nodes of my troubled waves –
Into my dark I have drawn down his light.

I weave upon the empty floor of space
The bridal dance, I dance the mysteries
That set the house of Pentheus ablaze –
His radiance shines into my darkest place.

He lays in my deep grave his deathless fires,
In me his flame springs fountain tree and heart,
Soars up from nature's bed in a bird's flight –
Into my dark I have drawn down his light.

My leaves draw down the sun with their green hands
And bind his rays into the world's wild rose.
I hold my mirroring seas before his face –
His radiance shines into my darkest place.

3

See, the clear sky is threaded with a thousand rays,
The birds' unseen but certain ways
That draw the swallow and the homing dove
As eyebeams overleap distances between stars.

Whistle of wings heralds oncoming spirit –
Life-bearing birds follow the bright invisible trace
That draws the skein of grey geese flying north
Or hangs the hawk at one point, motionless.
Life's ways pass through us, over us, beyond us.

Birds home to the house of the world, to the islands,
To ledges of sheer cliff, to wind-tossed tree-tops
To the high moorland where the lapwing builds –
Nest and grave are where the quick joy fails.

Their great and certain impulses are spent
In snowdrift, salt wave, dashed against rock-face,
But strong wings buffeted by wind and blizzard
Still follow the way that leads through storm to rest.

Bird angels, heavenly vehicles,
They die and are reborn – the bird is dust
But the deathless winged delight pursues its way.

Shining travellers from another dimension
Whose heaven-sent flight homes to the green earth,
What gossamer desire floats out to guide
Spirit ascending and descending between grave and sky?

4

LET in the wind
Let in the rain
Let in the moors tonight.

The storm beats on my window-pane,
Night stands at my bed-foot,
Let in the fear,
Let in the pain,
Let in the trees that toss and groan,
Let in the north tonight.

Let in the nameless formless power
That beats upon my door,
Let in the ice, let in the snow,
The banshee howling on the moor,
The bracken-bush on the bleak hillside,
Let in the dead tonight.

The whistling ghost behind the dyke,
The dead that rot in mire,
Let in the thronging ancestors
The unfulfilled desire,
Let in the wraith of the dead earl,
Let in the unborn tonight.

Let in the cold,
Let in the wet,
Let in the loneliness,
Let in the quick,
Let in the dead,
Let in the unpeopled skies.

Oh how can virgin fingers weave
A covering for the void,
How can my fearful heart conceive
Gigantic solitude?
How can a house so small contain
A company so great?
Let in the dark,
Let in the dead,
Let in your love tonight.

Let in the snow that numbs the grave,
Let in the acorn-tree,
The mountain stream and mountain stone,
Let in the bitter sea.

Fearful is my virgin heart
And frail my virgin form,
And must I then take pity on
The raging of the storm
That rose up from the great abyss
Before the earth was made,
That pours the stars in cataracts
And shakes this violent world?

Let in the fire,
Let in the power,
Let in the invading might.

Gentle must my fingers be
And pitiful my heart
Since I must bind in human form
A living power so great,
A living impulse great and wild

That cries about my house
With all the violence of desire
Desiring this my peace.

Pitiful my heart must hold
The lonely stars at rest,
Have pity on the raven's cry
The torrent and the eagle's wing,
The icy water of the tarn
And on the biting blast.

Let in the wound,
Let in the pain,
Let in your child tonight.

5

THE sleeper at the rowan's foot
Dreams the darkness at the root,
Dreams the flow that ascends the vein
And fills with world the dreamer's brain.

Wild tree filled with wind and rain
Day and night invade your dream,
Unseen brightness of the sun,
Waters flowing underground
Rise in bud and flower and shoot,
And the burden is so great
Of the dark flow from without,
Of sun streaming from the sky
And the dead rising from the root,
Of the earth's desire to be
In this dreaming incarnate
That world has overflowed the tree.

Oh do not wake, oh do not wake
The sleeper in the rowan's shade,
Mountains rest within his thought,
Clouds are drifting in his brain,

Snows upon his eyelids fall,
Winds are piping in his song,
Night is gathered at his root,
Stars are blossoming in his crown,
Storm without finds peace within,
World is resting in his dream.

Lonely dreamer on the hill
I have dreamed a thousand years,
I have dreamed returning spring,
Earth's delight and golden sun,
I have dreamed the pheasant's eye,
The heather and the flashing burn,
For the world has filled my dream:
Dream has overflowed the tree.

World without presses so sore
Upon the roots and branches fine
The dreamer can contain no more
And overflows in falling flowers,
Lets fall the bitter rowan fruit
Harsh as tears and bright as blood,
Berries that the wild birds eat
Till stripped of dream the sleeper lies,
Stripped of world the naked tree.
But on the hillside I have heard
The voice of the prophetic bird
That feeds upon the bitter fruit,
I have heard the blackbird sing
The wild music of the wind,
Utter the note the sun would cry,
Sing for the burn that flows away.

The sleeper of the rowan tree
As full of earth as dream can know,
As full of dream as tree can bear
Sends the bird singing in the air
As full of world as song can cry,
And yet the song is overflowed,

For pressing at the tree's deep root
Still underground, unformed, is world.

The invading world must break the dream
So heavy is the weight of sky,
So violent the water's flow
So vast the hills that would be born,
Beyond the utterance of bird
The mountain voice that would be sung,
The world of wild that would be man –
The dream has overflowed the tree.

6

THE window-panes grow dark, the walls recede,
Grow infinitely remote, and the familiar room
No longer houses me, no longer encloses;
House insubstantial into nothing dwindles,
I and the earth must part – and who am I
That with this dark winged messenger must fly
Into the soul's dark night?

I – who am I, that enter death's dimension?
I and this swift-winged bird-form have grown one,
My thought is fused with his thought, will with his will,
And we are one in purposes unknown
To bird or soul, human or angel mind,
And yet we go – the destination draws us.

As sleeper wakes from sleep, I wake from waking.
World's image fails and founders, mountain forms,
Garden and trees, heel over into darkness,
Go down the night like ice in northern ocean,
Nothing withholds house from crumbling, hills from falling.
Only the bird-flight, and this travelling
Of the soul into its own night, are certain.

House that has sheltered me since I was born,
Flowers and trees and skies and running burn,

Body of death I lifelong have been building,
My face, hands, voice, language and cast of thought
No longer me, or mine – I dreamed them into being,
Being that is unmade again into the night,
Grows tenuous, and is gone.

In the round barrow on the moor, a king's sword rusts
Under the cropped turf, necklace and golden cup
Lie in the finer dust of a dead queen,
And when the ghosts come blowing on the north wind
They find again the treasures that once seemed
Inseparable from their own living, underground
In the earth circle, in the bone's mound.

I too have haunted memories,
Places once loved, travelled back thirty years
To where home was, to find the hills still standing
To find the old stone house, the trees cut down,
But water still flowing from the village well
Where once I dipped my bucket as a child.
Even such returning desecrates –
Do not disturb the barrow on the hill,
Leave buried there the treasure of past days.

Not in overlong continuance see
Of amulet or ghost, in wraith of what has been,
Evidence of soul's immortality.
The ghost that haunts, the haunting memory
Is the continuance only of the dead.
Such earth-bound spirits, into soul's night unborn
Miss the one way to that destination
From which the homing soul knows no return.

Yet with what infinite gentleness being flows
Into the forms of nature, and unfolds
Into the slowly ascending tree of life
That opens, bud by bud, into the sky.
World, with what unending patience, grows,
Ascends the roots from the dark well of night

From stone to plant, from blind sense into sight
Up to the highest branch, where the raven head grows white.

But body was imperfect from the first,
Heart, sense, and the fine mesh of word and thought
Will not contain the abundance of the world.
The god that in the ascending tree, bird, stone,
River and mountain, wind and rain
Has remained hidden since the world began,
The power that overflows and shatters every form,
Calls on death to come, to break the imperfect mould.

Spirit, freed from the form into which you flowed,
Prisoned merlin of the groaning tree,
The self you were in nature falls away
All at once into dust, as the bird-heart homes.
Dark into dark, spirit into spirit flies,
Home, with not one dear image in the heart.

LOVE SPELL

By the travelling wind
By the restless clouds
By the space of the sky,

By the foam of the surf
By the curve of the wave
By the flowing of the tide,

By the way of the sun,
By the dazzle of light
By the path across the sea,
                    Bring my lover.

By the way of the air,
By the hoodie crow's flight
By the eagle on the wind,

By the cormorant's cliff
By the seal's rock
By the raven's crag,

By the shells on the strand
By the ripples on the sand
By the brown sea-wrack,
           Bring my lover.

By the mist and the rain
By the waterfall
By the running burn,

By the clear spring
By the holy well
And the fern by the pool
           Bring my lover.

By the sheepwalks on the hills
By the rabbit's tracks
By the stones of the ford,
           Bring my lover.

By the long shadow
By the evening light
By the midsummer sun
           Bring my lover.

By the scent of the white rose
Of the bog myrtle
And the scent of the thyme
           Bring my lover.

By the lark's song
By the blackbird's note
By the raven's croak
           Bring my lover.

By the voices of the air
By the water's song
By the song of a woman
           Bring my lover.

By the sticks burning on the hearth
By the candle's flame
By the fire in the blood
                Bring my lover.

By the touch of hands
By the meeting of lips
By love's unrest
                Bring my lover.

By the quiet of the night
By the whiteness of my breast
By the peace of sleep
                Bring my lover.

By the blessing of the dark
By the beating of the heart
By my unborn child,
                Bring my lover.

SPELL AGAINST SORROW

Who will take away
Carry away sorrow,
Bear away grief?

Stream wash away
Float away sorrow,
Flow away, bear away
Wear away sorrow,
Carry away grief.

Mists hide away
Shroud my sorrow,
Cover the mountains,
Overcloud remembrance,
Hide away grief.

Earth take away
Make away sorrow,
Bury the lark's bones
Under the turf.
Bury my grief.

Black crow tear away
Rend away sorrow,
Talon and beak
Pluck out the heart
And the nerves of pain,
Tear away grief.

Sun take away
Melt away sorrow,
Dew lies grey,
Rain hangs on the grass,
Sun dry tears.

Sleep take away
Make away sorrow,
Take away the time,
Fade away place,
Carry me away
From the world of my sorrow.

Song sigh away
Breathe away sorrow,
Words tell away,
Spell away sorrow,
Charm away grief.

SPELL TO BRING LOST CREATURES HOME

HOME, home,
Wild birds home!
Lark to the grass,
Wren to the hedge,
Rooks to the tree-tops,
Swallow to the eaves,
Eagle to its crag
And raven to its stone,
All birds home!

Home, home,
Strayed ones home,
Rabbit to burrow
Fox to earth,
Mouse to the wainscot,
Rat to the barn,
Cattle to the byre,
Dog to the hearth,
All beasts home!

Home, home,
Wanderers home,
Cormorant to rock
Gulls from the storm,
Boat to the harbour
Safe sail home!

Children home,
At evening home,
Boys and girls
From the roads come home,
Out of the rain
Sons come home,
From the gathering dusk,
Young ones home!

Home, home,
All souls home,
Dead to the graveyard,
Living to the lamplight,
Old to the fireside,
Girls from the twilight,
Babe to the breast
And heart to its haven,
Lost ones home!

SPELL OF CREATION

WITHIN the flower there lies a seed,
Within the seed there springs a tree,
Within the tree there spreads a wood.

In the wood there burns a fire,
And in the fire there melts a stone,
Within the stone a ring of iron.

Within the ring there lies an O
Within the O there looks an eye,
In the eye there swims a sea,

And in the sea reflected sky,
And in the sky there shines the sun,
Within the sun a bird of gold.

Within the bird there beats a heart,
And from the heart there flows a song,
And in the song there sings a word.

In the word there speaks a world,
A word of joy, a world of grief,
From joy and grief there springs my love.

Oh love, my love, there springs a world,
And on the world there shines a sun
And in the sun there burns a fire,

Within the fire consumes my heart
And in my heart there beats a bird,
And in the bird there wakes an eye,

Within the eye, earth, sea and sky,
Earth, sky and sea within an O
Lie like the seed within the flower.

THE UNLOVED

I AM pure loneliness
I am empty air
I am drifting cloud.

I have no form
I am boundless
I have no rest.

I have no house
I pass through places
I am indifferent wind.

I am the white bird
Flying away from land
I am the horizon.

I am a wave
That will never reach the shore

I am an empty shell
Cast up on the sand.

I am the moonlight
On the cottage with no roof.

I am the forgotten dead
In the broken vault on the hill.

I am the old man
Carrying his water in a pail.

I am light
Travelling in empty space.

I am a diminishing star
Speeding away
Out of the universe.

AMO ERGO SUM

BECAUSE I love
    The sun pours out its rays of living gold
    Pours out its gold and silver on the sea.

Because I love
    The earth upon her astral spindle winds
    Her ecstasy-producing dance.

Because I love
    Clouds travel on the winds through wide skies,
    Skies wide and beautiful, blue and deep.

Because I love
    Wind blows white sails,
    The wind blows over flowers, the sweet wind blows.

Because I love
    The ferns grow green, and green the grass, and green
    The transparent sunlit trees.

Because I love
    Larks rise up from the grass
    And all the leaves are full of singing birds.

Because I love
    The summer air quivers with a thousand wings,
    Myriads of jewelled eyes burn in the light.

Because I love
    The iridescent shells upon the sand
    Take forms as fine and intricate as thought.

Because I love
    There is an invisible way across the sky,
    Birds travel by that way, the sun and moon
    And all the stars travel that path by night.

Because I love
    There is a river flowing all night long.

Because I love
    All night the river flows into my sleep,
    Ten thousand living things are sleeping in my arms,
    And sleeping wake, and flowing are at rest.

SPELL OF SLEEP

LET him be safe in sleep
As leaves folded together
As young birds under wings
As the unopened flower.

Let him be hidden in sleep
As islands under rain,
As mountains within their clouds,
As hills in the mantle of dusk.

Let him be free in sleep
As the flowing tides of the sea,
As the travelling wind on the moor,
As the journeying stars in space.

Let him be upheld in sleep
As a cloud at rest on the air,
As sea-wrack under the waves
When the flowing tide covers all

And the shells' delicate lives
Open on the sea-floor.

Let him be healed in sleep
In the quiet waters of night
In the mirroring pool of dreams
Where memory returns in peace,
Where the troubled spirit grows wise
And the heart is comforted.

SPELL OF SAFEKEEPING

WINGS over nest
Shelter and hide
From mouths of night,

Rose with green
Calyx enclose
From storm and rain,

Lid over eye,
Intangible dream,
Cover the sky.

Arms enfold
Lover and child,
Safe withhold
Flesh and blood
From dread of dark
And death by day.

TWO INVOCATIONS OF DEATH

DEATH, I repent
Of these hands and feet
That for forty years
Have been my own
And I repent
Of flesh and bone,
Of heart and liver,
Of hair and skin –
Rid me, death,
Of face and form,
Of all that I am.

And I repent
Of the forms of thought,
The habit of mind
And heart crippled
By long-spent pain,
The memory-traces
Faded and worn
Of vanished places
And human faces
Not rightly seen
Or understood,
Rid me, death,
Of the words I have used.

Not this or that
But all is amiss,
That I have done,
And I have seen
Sin and sorrow
Befoul the world –
Release me, death,
Forgive, remove

From place and time
The trace of all
That I have been.

2

FROM a place I came
That was never in time,
From the beat of a heart
That was never in pain.
The sun and the moon,
The wind and the world,
The song and the bird
Travelled my thought
Time out of mind.
Shall I know at last
My lost delight?

Tell me, death,
How long must I sorrow
My own sorrow?
While I remain
The world is ending,
Forests are falling,
Suns are fading,
While I am here
Now is ending
And in my arms
The living are dying.
Shall I come at last
To the lost beginning?

Words and words
Pour through my mind
Like sand in the shell
Of the ear's labyrinth,
The desert of brain's
Cities and solitudes,

Dreams, speculations
And vast forgetfulness.
Shall I learn at last
The lost meaning?

Oh my lost love
I have seen you fly
Away like a bird,
As a fish elude me,
A stone ignore me,
In a tree's maze
You have closed against me
The spaces of earth,
Prolonged to the stars'
Infinite distances,
With strange eyes
You have not known me,
Thorn you have wounded,
Fire you have burned
And talons torn me.
How long must I bear
Self and identity –
Shall I find at last
My lost being?

MESSAGE

Look, beloved child, into my eyes, see there
Your self, mirrored in that living water
From whose deep pools all images of earth are born.
See, in the gaze that holds you dear
All that you were, are, and shall be for ever.
In recognition beyond time and seeming
Love knows the face that each soul turns towards heaven.

LAMENT

WHERE are those dazzling hills touched by the sun,
Those crags in childhood that I used to climb?
Hidden, hidden under mist is yonder mountain,
Hidden is the heart.

A day of cloud, a lifetime falls between,
Gone are the heather moors and the pure stream,
Gone are the rocky places and the green,
Hidden, hidden under sorrow is yonder mountain.

Oh storm and gale of tears, whose blinding screen
Makes weather of grief, snow's drifting curtain
Palls the immortal heights once seen.
Hidden is the heart.

A WORD KNOWN TO THE DEAD

I WATCH white hills grow pale as empty air,
Cold draught of space blows the drifting snow,
The grey stone boundaries fade, and the sun darkens.

I watch an ash-tree stand bared to the sky
As void of being as the invisible air
That cannot bind or bend the rainbow from the darkness.

Winter how many birds' bright eyes has frozen
Into a dark gaze, and dead wild creatures stare
With open eyes upon the dazzling hills,
Eyes vacant as interstellar space, where light is darkness.

Tree's branches faint and flicker from the eye,
There is no road, earth fails beneath my feet
And the hardest rock in the hills is hollow as night,

For I have heard
A certain cold word spoken in the heart,
A word that the dead hear and obey in darkness.

THREE POEMS ON ILLUSION

1. THE MIRAGE

No, I have seen the mirage tremble, seen how thin
The veil stretched over apparaent time and space
To make the habitable earth, the enclosed garden.

I saw on a bare hillside an ash-tree stand
And all its intricate branches suddenly
Failed, as I gazed, to be a tree,
And road and hillside failed to make a world.
Hill, tree, sky, distance, only seemed to be
And I saw nothing I could give a name,
Not any name known to the heart.

What failed? The retina received
The differing waves of light, or rays of darkness,
Eyes, hands, all senses brought me
Messages that lifelong I had believed.
Appearances that once composed reality
Here turned to dust, to mist, to motes in the eye
Or like the reflection broken on a pool
The unrelated visual fragments foundered
On a commotion of those deeps
Where earth floats safe, when waves are still.

The living instrument
When fingers gently touch the strings,
Or when a quiet wind
Blows through the reed, makes music of birds,
Song, words, the human voice.
Too strong a blast from outer space,
A blow too heavy breaks and silences
The singer and the song;
A grief too violent
Wrecks the image of the world, on waves whose amplitude
Beats beyond the compass of the heart.

The waves subside, the image reassembles:
There was a tree once more, hills, and the world,

But I have seen the emptiness of air
Ready to swallow up the bird in its flight,
Or note of music, or winged word, the void
That traps the rabbit on cropped turf as in a snare,
Lies at the heart of the wren's warm living eggs,
In pollen dust of summer flowers, opens
Within the smallest seed of grass, the abyss
That now and always underlies the hills.

2. The Instrument

Death, and it is broken,
The delicate apparatus of the mind,
Tactile, sensitive to light, responsive to sound,
The soul's instrument, tuned to earth's music,
Vibrant to all the waves that break on the shores of the world.

Perhaps soul only puts out a hand,
Antenna or pseudopodium, an extended touch
To receive the spectrum of colour, and the lower octave of pain,
Reaches down into the waves of nature
As a child dips an arm into the sea,
And death is the withdrawal of attention
That has discovered all it needs to know,
Or, if not all, enough for now,
If not enough, something to bear in mind.

And it may be that soul extends
Organs of sense
Tuned to waves here scarcely heard, or only
Heard distantly in dreams,
Worlds other otherwise than as stars,
Asteroids and suns are distant, in natural space.
The supersonic voices of angels reach us
Even now, and we touch one another
Sometimes, in love, with hands that are not hands,
With immaterial substance, with a body
Of interfusing thought, a living eye,
Spirit that passes unhindered through walls of stone
And walks upon those waves that we call ocean.

3. Exile

THEN, I had no doubt
That snowdrops, violets, all creatures, I myself
Were lovely, were loved, were love.
Look, they said,
And I had only to look deep into the heart,
Dark, deep into the violet, and there read,
Before I knew of any word for flower or love,
The flower, the love, the word.

They never wearied of telling their being; and I
Asked of the rose, only more rose, the violet
More violet; untouched by time
No flower withered or flame died,
But poised in its own eternity, until the looker moved
On to another flower, opening its entity.

I see them now across a void
Wider and deeper than time and space.
All that I have come to be
Lies between my heart and the rose,
The flame, the bird, the blade of grass.
The flowers are veiled;
And in a shadow-world, appearances
Pass across a great *toile vide*
Where the image flickers, vanishes,
Where nothing is, but only seems.
But still the mind, curious to pursue
Long followed them, as they withdrew
Deep within their inner distances,
Pulled the petals from flowers, the wings from flies,
Hunted the heart with a dissecting-knife
And scattered under a lens the dust of life;
But the remoter, stranger
Scales iridescent, cells, spindles, chromosomes,
Still merely are:
With hail, snow-crystals, mountains, stars,
Fox in the dusk, lightning, gnats in the evening air

They share the natural mystery,
Proclaim I AM, and remain nameless.

Sometimes from far away
They sign to me;
A violet smiles from the dim verge of darkness,
A raindrop hangs beckoning on the eaves,
And once, in long wet grass,
A young bird looked at me.
Their being is lovely, is love;
And if my love could cross the desert self
That lies between all that I am and all that is,
They would forgive and bless.

THE HOLY SHROUD

FACE of the long-dead
Floating up from under the deep waves
Of time, that we try to see,
To draw towards us by closer looking, that fades
And will not become more clear than shadow,
Mist gathering always like dusk round a dead king,
That face, however closely we look, is always departing,
Neither questions nor answers us. It is still,
It is whole, has known, loved, suffered all,
And un-known all again.
That face of man
Un-knows us now – whatever being passed
Beyond that holy shroud into the mind of God
No longer sees this earth: we are alone.

THREE POEMS OF INCARNATION

1

At the day's end I found

Nightfall wrapped about a stone.

I took the cold stone in my hand,
The shadowy surfaces of life unwound,
And within I found
A bird's fine bone.

I warmed the relic in my hand
Until a living heart
Beat, and the tides flowed
Above, below, within.

There came a boat riding the storm of blood
And in the boat a child,

In the boat a child
Riding the waves of song,
Riding the waves of pain.

2. INVOCATION

Child in the little boat
Come to the land
Child of the seals
Calf of the whale
Spawn of the octopus
Fledgeling of cormorant
Gannet and herring-gull,
Come from the sea,
Child of the sun,
Son of the sky.
Safely pass
The mouths of the water,

The mouths of night,
The teeth of the rocks,
The mouths of the wind,
Safely float
On the dangerous waves
Of an ocean sounding
Deeper than red
Darker than violet,
Safely cross
The ground-swell of pain
Of the waves that break
On the shores of the world.

Life everlasting
Love has prepared
The paths of your coming.
Plankton and nekton
Free-swimming pelagic
Spawn of the waters
Has brought you to birth
In the life-giving pools,
Spring has led you
Over the meadows
In fox's fur
Has nestled and warmed you,
With the houseless hare
In the rushes has sheltered,
Warm under feathers
Of brooding wings
Safe has hidden
In the grass secretly
Clothed in disguise
Of beetle and grasshopper
Small has laid you
Under a stone
In the nest of the ants
Myriadfold scattered
In pollen of pine forests

Set you afloat
Like dust on the air
And winged in multitudes
Hatched by the sun
From the mud of rivers.
Newborn you have lain
In the arms of mothers,
You have drawn life
From a myriad breasts,
The mating of animals
Has not appalled you,
The longing of lovers
You have not betrayed,
You have come unscathed
From the field of battle
From famine and plague
You have lived undefiled
In the gutters of cities
We have seen you dancing
Barefoot in villages,
You have been to school
But kept your wisdom.

Child in the little boat,
Come to the land,
Child of the seals.

3

WHO stands at my door in the storm and rain
On the threshold of being?
One who waits till you call him in
From the empty night.

Are you a stranger, out in the storm,
Or has my enemy found me out
On the edge of being?

I am no stranger who stands at the door
Nor enemy come in the secret night,
I am your child, in darkness and fear
On the verge of being.

Go back, my child, to the rain and the storm,
For in this house there is sorrow and pain
In the lonely night.

I will not go back for sorrow or pain,
For my true love weeps within
And waits for my coming.

Go back, my babe, to the vacant night
For in this house dwell sin and hate
On the verge of being.

I will not go back for hate or sin,
I will not go back for sorrow or pain,
For my true love mourns within
On the threshold of night.

THE VICTIMS

For G.M.

THEY walk towards us willingly and gently,
Unblemished, the white kid, the calf,
Their newborn coats scarcely dry from the natal waters.
Each hair lies in its new place, ripple-marked
By the rhythms of growth, the tides
That washed them up onto the shores of time.

Their young eyes, unsurprised, look towards us,
We see them stand, beautiful, on spring grass
Knowing that the upgathering of perfect form must pass,
Those intricate knots of ganglia and veins,
The rhythmic heart, the breath of life.
We first receive their wounding in our hearts

With all the inexpressible guilt of love;
For the first worshipping touch of our tragic hands must soil
And trouble the unconscious unicorn
That does not even know it stands on earth.
We offer them bunches of buttercups and spring grass
With all the inexpressible love of guilt:
We strike, even as we look,
The first wound of sacrifice.

THE COMPANY

So many gathered in my room last night.
I felt them close all round me, existences,
Living presences, invisible essences,
Each centred in its own peculiar secret joy,
Each joy given being by a peculiar wisdom
Pertaining to its nature like a dimension,
Or like a world, enclosed within a spirit,
But none a spirit enclosed within a world.

Not in the world, and yet they gathered in my room;
Some stood still, inside the door, some
Thronged the firelight and the shadows; some hung
Like resting birds, in the curtains, perched high
On the bookshelves, poised on the opening flowers
Of a hyacinth, others hid in their own fiery darkness.

Where had they come from?
Out of my joy, out of my sorrow,
Living entities sprung into life from the dust
Of my existence, taking wing, making song?
Or were they there already before I came
Alone into my room, waiting
Until my joy should open eyes to see them,
Until my sorrow should reach down
Into the depths of being, and there find them,
Find such a company of living multitude?

SEVENTH DAY

PASSIVE I lie, looking up through leaves,
An eye only, one of the eyes of earth
That open at a myriad points at the living surface.
Eyes that earth opens see and delight
Because of the leaves, because of the unfolding of the leaves.
The folding, veining, imbrication, fluttering, resting,
The green and deepening manifold of the leaves.

Eyes of the earth know only delight
Untroubled by anything that I am, and I am nothing:
All that nature is, receive and recognize,
Pleased with the sky, the falling water and the flowers,
With bird and fish and the striations of stone.
Every natural form, living and moving
Delights these eyes that are no longer mine
That open upon earth and sky pure vision.
Nature sees, sees itself, is both seer and seen.

This is the divine repose, that watches
The ever-changing light and shadow, rock and sky and ocean.

THE MARRIAGE OF PSYCHE

1. THE HOUSE

IN my love's house
There are hills and pastures carpeted with flowers,
His roof is the blue sky, his lamp the evening star,
The doors of his house are the winds, and the rain his curtain.
In his house are many mountains, each alone,
And islands where the sea-birds home.

In my love's house
There is a waterfall that flows all night
Down from the mountain summit where the snow lies
White in the shimmering blue of everlasting summer,

Down from the high crag where the eagle flies.
At his threshold the tides of ocean rise,
And the porpoise follows the shoals into still bays
Where starfish gleam on brown weed under still water.

In sleep I was borne here
And waking found rivers and waves my servants,
Sun and cloud and winds, bird-messengers,
And all the flocks of his hills and shoals of his seas.
I rest, in the heat of the day, in the light shadow of leaves
And voices of air and water speak to me.
All this he has given me, whose face I have never seen,
But into whose all-enfolding arms I sink in sleep.

2. THE RING

He has married me with a ring, a ring of bright water
Whose ripples travel from the heart of the sea,
He has married me with a ring of light, the glitter
Broadcast on the swift river.
He has married me with the sun's circle
Too dazzling to see, traced in summer sky.
He has crowned me with the wreath of white cloud
That gathers on the snowy summit of the mountain,
Ringed me round with the world-circling wind,
Bound me to the whirlwind's centre.
He has married me with the orbit of the moon
And with the boundless circle of the stars,
With the orbits that measure years, months, days and nights,
Set the tides flowing,
Commands the winds to travel or be at rest.

At the ring's centre,
Spirit, or angel troubling the still pool,
Causality not in nature,
Finger's touch that summons at a point, a moment
Stars and planets, life and light
Or gathers cloud about an apex of cold,
Transcendent touch of love summons my world to being.

[93]

SHELLS

REACHING down arm-deep into bright water
I gathered on white sand under waves
Shells, drifted up on beaches where I alone
Inhabit a finite world of years and days.
I reached my arm down a myriad years
To gather treasure from the yester-millennial sea-floor,
Held in my fingers forms shaped on the day of creation.

Building their beauty in the three dimensions
Over which the world recedes away from us,
And in the fourth, that takes away ourselves
From moment to moment and from year to year
From first to last they remain in their continuous present.
The helix revolves like a timeless thought,
Instantaneous from apex to rim
Like a dance whose figure is limpet or murex, cowrie or
     golden winkle.

They sleep on the ocean floor like humming-tops
Whose music is the mother-of-pearl octave of the rainbow,
Harmonious shells that whisper for ever in our ears,
'The world that you inhabit has not yet been created.'

ROCK

THERE is stone in me that knows stone,
Substance of rock that remembers the unending unending
Simplicity of rest
While scorching suns and ice ages
Pass over rock-face swiftly as days.
In the longest time of all come the rock's changes,
Slowest of all rhythms, the pulsations
That raise from the planet's core the mountain ranges
And weather them down to sand on the sea-floor.

Remains in me record of rock's duration.
My ephemeral substance was still in the veins of the earth from
    the beginning,
Patient for its release, not questioning
When, when will come the flowering, the flowing,
The pulsing, the awakening, the taking wing,
The long longed-for night of the bridegroom's coming.

There is stone in me that knows stone,
Whose sole state is stasis
While the slow cycle of the stars whirls a world of rock
Through light-years where in nightmare I fall crying
'Must I travel fathomless distance for ever and ever?'
All that is in me of the rock, replies
'For ever, if it must be: be, and be still; endure.'

WATER

THERE is a stream that flowed before the first beginning
Of bounding form that circumscribes
Protophyte and protozoon.
The passive permeable sea obeys,
Reflects, rises and falls as forces of moon and wind
Draw this way or that its weight of waves;
But the mutable water holds no trace
Of crest or ripple or whirlpool; the wave breaks,
Scatters in a thousand instantaneous drops
That fall in sphere and ovoid, film-spun bubbles
Upheld in momentary equilibrium of strain and stress
In the ever-changing network woven between stars.

When, in the flux, the first bounding membrane
Forms, like the memory-trace of a preceding state,
When the linked organic chain
Holds against current and tide its microcosm,
Of man's first disobedience, what first cause

[95]

Impresses with inherent being
Entities, selves, globules, vase-shapes, vortices,
Amoeboid, ovoid, pulsing or ciliate,
That check the flow of waters like forms of thought,
Pause, poised in the unremembering current –
By what will to be fathered in the primal matrix?
The delicate tissue of life retains, bears
The stigmata, the trace, the signature, endures
The tension of the formative moment, withstands
The passive downward deathward streaming,
Leaps the falls, a salmon ascending, a tree growing.
But still the stream that flows down to stillness
Seeks the end-all of all waters,
Welcomes all solving, dissolving, undoing,
Returns, loses itself, loses self and bounds,
Body, identity, memory, sinks to forgetfulness,
The state of unknowing, unbeing,
The flux that precedes all life, that we reassume, dying,
Ceasing to trouble the flowing of things with the fleeting
Dream and hope and despair of this transient perilous selving.

THE MOMENT

NEVER, never again
This moment, never
These slow ripples
Across smooth water,
Never again these
Clouds white and grey
In sky sharp crystalline
Blue as the tern's cry
Shrill in light air
Salt from the ocean,
Sweet from flowers.

Here coincide
The long histories
Of forms recurrent
That meet at a point
And part in a moment,
The rapid waves
Of wind and water
And slower rhythm
Of rock weathering
And land sinking.

In teeming pools
The life cycle
Of brown weed
Is intersecting
The frequencies
Of diverse shells
Each with its variant
Arc or spiral
Spun from a point
In tone and semitone
Of formal octave.

Here come soaring
White gulls
Leisurely wheeling
In air over islands
Sea pinks and salt grass,
Gannet and eider,
Curlew and cormorant
Each a differing
Pattern of ecstasy
Recurring at nodes
In an on-flowing current,
The perpetual species,
Repeated, renewed
By the will of joy
In eggs lodged safe
On perilous ledges.

The sun that rises
Upon one earth
Sets on another.
Swiftly the flowers
Are waxing and waning,
The tall yellow iris
Unfolds its corolla
As primroses wither,
Scrolls of fern
Unroll and midges
Dance for an hour
In the evening air,
The brown moth
From its pupa emerges
And the lark's bones
Fall apart in the grass.

The sun that rose
From the sea this morning
Will never return,
For the broadcast light
That brightens the leaves
And glances on water
Will travel tonight
On its long journey
Out of the universe,
Never this sun,
This world, and never
Again this watcher.

THE LOCKED GATES

EVERYWHERE the substance of earth is the gate that we cannot pass.
Seek in Hebridean isles lost paradise,
There is yet the heaviness of water, the heaviness of stone
And the heaviness of the body I bring to this inviolate place.
Foot sinks in bog as I gather white water-lilies in the tarn,
The knee is bruised on rock, and the wind is always blowing.
The locked gates of the world are the world's elements,
For the rocks of the beautiful hills hurt, and the silver seas drown,
Wind scores deep record of time on the weathered boulders,
The bird's hot heart consumes the soaring life to feather and bone,
And heather and asphodel crumble to peat that smoulders on
    crofters' fires.

MESSAGE FROM HOME

Do you remember, when you were first a child,
Nothing in the world seemed strange to you?
You perceived, for the first time, shapes already familiar,
And seeing, you knew that you had always known
The lichen on the rock, fern-leaves, the flowers of thyme,
As if the elements newly met in your body,
Caught up into the momentary vortex of your living
Still kept the knowledge of a former state,
In you retained recollection of cloud and ocean,
The branching tree, the dancing flame.

Now when nature's darkness seems strange to you,
And you walk, an alien, in the streets of cities,
Remember earth breathed you into her with the air, with the
    sun's rays,
Laid you in her waters asleep, to dream
With the brown trout among the milfoil roots,
From substance of star and ocean fashioned you,

[99]

At the same source conceived you
As sun and foliage, fish and stream.

Of all created things the source is one,
Simple, single as love; remember
The cell and seed of life, the sphere
That is, of child, white bird, and small blue dragon-fly
Green fern, and the gold four-petalled tormentilla
The ultimate memory.
Each latent cell puts out a future,
Unfolds its differing complexity
As a tree puts forth leaves, and spins a fate
Fern-traced, bird-feathered, or fish-scaled.
Moss spreads its green film on the moist peat,
The germ of dragon-fly pulses into animation and takes wing
As the water-lily from the mud ascends on its ropy stem
To open a sweet white calyx to the sky.
Man, with farther to travel from his simplicity,
From the archaic moss, fish, and lily parts,
And into exile travels his long way.

As you leave Eden behind you, remember your home,
For as you remember back into your own being
You will not be alone; the first to greet you
Will be those children playing by the burn,
The otters will swim up to you in the bay,
The wild deer on the moor will run beside you.
Recollect more deeply, and the birds will come,
Fish rise to meet you in their silver shoals,
And darker, stranger, more mysterious lives
Will throng about you at the source
Where the tree's deepest roots drink from the abyss.

Nothing in that abyss is alien to you.
Sleep at the tree's root, where the night is spun
Into the stuff of worlds, listen to the winds,
The tides, and the night's harmonies, and know
All that you knew before you began to forget,
Before you became estranged from your own being,

Before you had too long parted from those other
More simple children, who have stayed at home
In meadow and island and forest, in sea and river.
Earth sends a mother's love after her exiled son,
Entrusting her message to the light and the air,
The wind and waves that carry your ship, the rain that falls,
The birds that call to you, and all the shoals
That swim in the natal waters of her ocean.

The Hollow Hill

(1965)

Consider men as in a subterraneous habitation, resembling a cave, with its entrance expanding to the light . . ..
Suppose them to have been in this cave from their
childhood, with chains both on their legs and necks, so
as to remain there, and only able to look before them,
but by the chain incapable to turn their heads round . . ..

NIGHT THOUGHT

My soul and I last night
Looked down together.
I said, 'Here we are come
To the worst. Look down
That chasm where all has fallen,
The rose-bush and the garden
And the ancestral hills,
Every remembered stone.
Of that first house
There is no trace, none.
You'll never cross that burn,
Again, nor the white strand
Where lifted from the deep
Shells lie upon the sand
Or among sea-pinks blown,
Never hear again
Those wild sea-voices call,
Eider and gull rejoicing.
Turn away, turn
From the closed door of home,
You live there no longer,
Nor shall again.
You have no place at all
Anywhere on earth
That is your own, and none
Calls you back again.'

Soul said, 'Before you were
I spanned the abyss:
Freedom it is, unbounded,
Unbounded laughter. Come!'

EUDAIMON

BOUND and free,
I to you, you to me,
We parted at the gate
Of childhood's house, I bound,
You free to ebb and flow
In that life-giving sea
In whose dark womb
I drowned.

In a dark night
In flight unbounded
You bore me bound
To my prison-house,
Whose window invisible bars
From mine your world.

Your life my death
Weeps in the night
Your freedom bound
To me, though bound still free
To leave my tomb,

On wings invisible
To span the night and all the stars,
Pure liquid and serene,
I you, you me,
There one; on earth alone
I lie, you free.

NIGHT SKY

THERE came such clear opening of the night sky,
The deep glass of wonders, the dark mind
In unclouded gaze of the abyss
Opened like the expression of a face.

I looked into that clarity where all things are
End and beginning, and saw
My destiny there: 'So', I said, 'no other
Was possible ever. This
Is I. The pattern stands so for ever.'

What am I? Bound and bounded,
A pattern among the stars, a point in motion
Tracing my way. I am my way: it is I
I travel among the wonders.
Held in that gaze and known
In the eye of the abyss,
'Let it be so,' I said,
And my heart laughed with joy
To know the death I must die.

KORE IN HADES

I CAME, yes, dear, dear
Mother for you I came, so I remember,
To lie in your warm
Bed, to watch the wonder flame:
Burning, golden gentle and bright the light of the living.

With you I ran
To see the roadside green
Leaves and small cool bindweed flowers
Living rejoicing to proclaim
We are, we are manifold, in multitude
We come, we are near and far,
Past and future innumerable, we are yours,
We are you. I listened
To the sweet bird whose song is for ever,
I was the little girl of the one mother.

World you wove me to please a child,
Yet its texture was thinner than light, fleeter
Than flame that burned while it seemed
Leaves and flowers and garden world without end.
Bright those faces closed and were over.

Here and now is over, the garden
Lost from time, its sun its moon
Mother, daughter, daughter, mother, never
Is now: there is nothing, nothing for ever.

ROSE

GATHER while you may
Vapour of water, dust of earth, rose
Of air and water and light that comes and goes:
Over and over again the rose is woven.

Who knows the beginning?
In the vein in the sun in the rain
In the rock in the light in the night there is none.
What moves light over water? An impulse
Of rose like the delight of girl's breasts
When the nipples bud and grow a woman
Where was a child, a woman to bear
A child unbegun (is there
Anywhere one? Are the people of dreams
Waiting – where? – to be born?) Does the green
Bud rose without end contain?
Within green sepals, green cells, you find none.
The crude
Moist, hard, green and cold
Petal on petal unfolding rose from nowhere.

But the perfect form is moving
Through time, the rose is a transit, a wave that weaves
Water, and petals fall like notes in order;
No more rose on ground unbecome

[108]

Unwoven unwound are dust are formless
And the rose is over but where
Labours for ever the weaver of roses?

BHEINN NAOMH

For Mary and John-Donald Macleod

1. SUN

SUN
Flashed from blades of salix of chitin of stone
Quiver of light on heather on hill on wings
Trembling makes one dazzling noon
Mirrored in rings of light that pulse in the burn
Glowing in eyes, throbbing in dust
Of butterflies dark as peat-pool brown
Endured in nerve, in ganglion in vein,
Budding of wings, leafing of lives
Myriadfold poised fragile on dark world lit with sight
Streaming undimmed, we suffer your joy
Poured down, down on in dark pools under
Overshadow of alder in undoing water.

2. GOLDEN FLOWERS

I HAVE travelled so far that I have come to the waterfall of Sgriol:
Curtain of mist, of netted leaves, inviolate leafy vale,
Fragrant veil of green-gold birch and song of the green-gold linnet,
A shadow withdrawn I enter for ever the sun-filled gloaming of Sgriol.

Light you have travelled so far out of the boundless void
From beyond the Isle of Skye over the sound of Sleat
You have laid a path of wonder over the bright sea
And touched with your finger the golden summit of Sgriol.

[109]

Water you have gathered in mist high over ben Sgriol,
So fast your drifting curtain of rain has fallen
That the noise of the sun-brown burn is filling the glen of Sgriol.

Seed you have grown so fast from the mould of the dead
You have unfolded a hundred flowers with golden petals,
The hundred-petalled golden flowers are filled with light
And leaves are moist with the life-giving waters of the burn of Sgriol.

Oh sun and water and green-gold flowers, I was here and now in the
    glen of Sgriol.

Light how fast you have travelled on into the abyss
And into ocean the burn that played in the sun lit fern of Sgriol.
Seed of miraculous flowers lies cold in the bog,
Sun sets in the beautiful land of the dead beyond the Isle of Skye.

3. THE LOCH

HIGH, high and still
Pale water mirrors
Thin air and still the high
Summit at rest in white
Water-spaces empty as thought.
The reeds wait
For ripple to trouble
Unsleeping gaze.
Nothing below it knows
But gathers the waters
That overflow
From the brim of reflection
Not all falls
Soul remains
High and lonely
While blood runs
Down by the easy
Ways of sorrow.

4. THE SUMMIT

FARTHER than I have been
All is changed: no water for moist souls,
Wind and stone is the world of the summit, stone and rain,
Stone, wind and cold, only the oldest things remain,
And wind unceasing has blown,
Without beginning or ending the wind has blown.
Noise of wind on rock cries to the soul 'Away,
Away, what wilt thou do?' The butterfly
Blown up against the summit meets the snow.
Those who rise there endure
Dragon of stone and dragon of air – by wind irresistible
Hurled, or still as stone, the long way
A dream while the wing of a bird
Brushes a grain of quartz from the unmoved hill.

5. MAN

MAN on the mountain listens to star and stone:
Memory of earth and heaven
Lies open on the hill; sun, moon and blood tell all.
The lonely voice that cried in the beginning
Calls in the belling of deer
And over the frozen loch unearthly music of the swan.
Thoughts of the dead are never silent
By the green mounds where houses stood,
Love and sorrow to come makes the air tremble.
Close as heartbeat is the word of the mountain,
Unsleeping the sky whose sight embraces all.

CHILDHOOD MEMORY

Sunshine in morning field,
Sunshining king-cups,
My flowers, my sun –
'But you cannot look at the sun,
No-one can look into the sun.'
And I said, 'I can,
I can, it is golden, it is mine,'
And looked into a dancing ball of blood,
A pulsing darkness blind with blood.

Sunshine in morning field,
Sunshining king-cups,
My sun, my flowers –
'But you cannot gather those flowers,
The calyx in your hand is speed, is power,
Is multitude – in grain of golden dust
Smaller than point of needle, there they dance,
Unnumbered constellations as the stars
They spin, they whirl, their infinitesimal space
Empty as night where suns burn out in space.'

Dear and familiar face
That beamed on childhood,
Shining on morning field and flower smile
What emptiness veiled,
Chasms of inhuman darkness veiled.

THAUMAS

Sometimes we see, one day, some day,
In a London street, in an obscure café,
A face we have known. 'That diviner of spirits,
If he can see auras, should have known who I am'
Said the young *sufi*, 'But he did not know me.'
I looked, and saw that you were no-one:

Your young face, gentle and grave, looked out of blue air
Like Krishna outlined in a flute-player,
Hovered like a reflection seen in water,
Trembling a little, for the waves never remain
Still for long enough to see quite clearly the image
Broken by cross and re-cross of ripples, torn
By the unrest of the great sea, shattered by the hurl
Of sorrow and rage that toss the wreckage.
Still in a calm or as the living wave slides past
The image is there for a moment,
Resting beautiful in the glass of wonders.
We look up and the sky is empty as always; only
Assembling the scattered for-ever broadcast light
Here, or there, in his creatures, is seen that Face.

LACHESIS

SOUL lonely comes and goes; for each our theme
We lonely must explore, lonely must dream
A story we each to ourselves must tell,
A book that as we read is written.

Our life a play of passion, says Raleigh's madrigal,
'Only we die, we die'; but older wisdom taught
That the dead change their garments and return,
Passing from sleep to sleep, from dream to dream.

In that life we dream, says Calderon, each soul
Is monster in the labyrinth of its own being.
Macbeth had his desire, an idiot's tale;
Yet the three fabulous spinners he had seen
Making from evil cause evil to come.

Oedipus' crime was greater, the murdered king
Where the three stories met being his father; yet
Blind when he saw, he came, a beggar and blind,
Honouring their mystery, to the gods
Whose life we die, living their death.

Dark lives are shades that make the picture bright,
Plotinus parabled; some born to sweet delight
And some to endless night, yet all are safe
As through those sweet or deadly dreams we pass,
Lost travellers all, Blake said; and Plato taught

That we ourselves have chosen what will befall.
In the Book of the Dead, the people of dreams,
By will and by compulsion drawn to birth
Live as punishment what each to live desires:
We are ourselves the evil dreams we suffer.

In what mind everlasting all is known,
Or in mind everlasting all forgotten
God knows, or maybe does not know, the Veda says;
Yet a few have seen the curtain drawn, and tell
With Juliana that all is well.

But what of that little bloodstained hand
Not all the bitter waves can wash,
Or the betraying hand dipped in the dish,
Predestined from the beginning of the world
And yet not guiltless, not forgiven?

Needs must these things be; and you and I,
My love, must suffer patiently what we are,
These parts of guilt and grief we play
Who must about our necks the millstone bear.

THE HOLLOW HILL

(Dun Aengus at Brugh na Boyne)

For Willa Muir

1

OUTSIDE, sun, frost, wind, rain,
Lichen, grass-root, bird-claw, scoring thorn
Wear away the stone that seals the tomb,
Erode the labyrinth inscribed in the stone,
Emblem of world and its unwinding
And inwinding volutions of the brain.
On the door out of the world the dead have left this sign.

The moving now has drawn its thread
Tracing the ravelled record of the dead
Through all the wanderings of the living.
Reaching at last the sum of our becoming,
The line inwound into a point again,
The spaces of the world full circle turn
Into the nought where all began.

We cannot look from the world into their house,
Or they look from their house into our sky;
For the low door where we crawl from world to world
Into the earth-cave bends and turns away
To close the hidden state of the dead from the light of day.
The grave is empty, they are gone:
In the last place they were, their clay
Clings crumbling to the roots of trees,
Whose fibres thread their way from earth to earth again.

Crouched in birth-posture in the cave
The ancestors are laid with the unborn,
(For who knows whether to die be not to live)
One worn hand touching the worn stone,
Calling the earth to witness, the other palm
Open to receive whatever falls:
Archaic icon of man's condition.

Yet so the great slabs have leaned three thousand years
That a single beam, shaft, arrow, ray
This dark house of the dead can pierce.
From world to world there is a needle's eye:
Light spans the heavens to find the punctum out,
To touch with finger of life a dead man's heart.

2

It is time, heart, to recall,
To recollect, regather all:
The grain is grown,
Reap what was sown
And bring into the barn your corn.

Those fields of childhood, tall
Meadow-grass and flowers small,
The elm whose dusky leaves
Patterned the sky with dreams innumerable
And labyrinthine vein and vine
And wandering tendrils green,
Have grown a seed so small
A single thought contains them all.

The white birds on their tireless wings return,
Spent feather, flesh and bone let fall,
And the blue distances of sea and sky
Close within the closing eye
As everywhere comes nowhere home.

Draw in my heart
Those golden rays whose threads of light
The visible veil of world have woven,
And through the needle's eye
Upon that river bright
Travels the laden sun
Back from its voyage through the night.

We depart and part,
We fail and fall
Till love calls home
All who our separate lonely ways have gone.

3

THE rock is written with the sign
In geometric diamond prison,
Prism, cube and rhomboid, mineral grain,
The frozen world of rigid form
Inexorable in line and plane
At every point where meet and part
The cross-ways of the enduring world.

In curving vault and delicate cone
Each formula of shell and bone
In willow-spray and branching vein,
In teleost's feathered skeleton,
In nerve of bird and human brain
Along its moving axis drawn
Each star of life has gone its way
Tracing the cross-ways of the world.

Here on death's door the hand of man
Has scored our history in the stone,
The emblematic branching tree
That crucifies to line and plane,
Writhes into life in nerve and vein,
Bleeds and runs and cowers and flies,
Resolved into a thought again
From nowhere come to nowhere gone
Those times and distances that span
The enduring cross-ways of the world.

THE tree of night is spangled with a thousand stars;
Plenum of inner spaces numberless
Of lives secret as leaves on night-elm,
Living maze of wisdom smaragdine
Opens in cell, in membrane, in chain in vein
Infinite number moving in waves that weave
In virgin vagina world-long forest of form,
Cold wild immaculate
Sanctuary of labyrinthine dream.
Lives throng the pleroma
Opening eyes and ears to listen:
Soft, soft they murmur mystery together.

O shadow-tree pinnate in a thousand leaf-ways,
Blades veined fine as insect-scales,
Glittering dust on soul's blue wing,
Full of eyes innumerable and senses fine
As feather green and the green linnet's song,
Arrow-swift wand in flight,
Pollen-grain on the wind
And bitter berry red,
Before you were, you are gone.

Gather a leaf blacker than night and bind it
Over the eye of the sun and the eye of the moon,
Closer than lid of blood, or lid of lead.
There is a banishing ritual for the world,
The great tree and its maze will shrivel
Smaller than pollen-grain, smaller than seed
Of bitter berry red: thought has no size at all;
And some in sorrow's well have seen
In daylight far stars glimmer pale.

WHITENESS of moonlight builds a house that is not there
On the bare hill,
Wide open house of night,
A gleaming house for those who are nowhere.

All there is valueless we value here,
Our houses are blacked out,
Things are dense darkness,
Nothing the silver surface of the night.
On black grass the untrodden dew is white,
On white birch black leaves glitter,
Bright rings scale the swift salmon river.

The house of the dead is alight,
The stones heaped over the cairn milk-white
In the mind's eye.
They say the charnel-house is a fairy-rath
But none knows where the dead are gone;
Yet when we turn away from a new grave
There is a lightness and a brightness
From those who have passed through the door that is nowhere.
Their death is over and done.
Ours still to come,
Grievous and life-long.
Not to be what we are,
Is it to be less, or more?
Waking, or dream, or dreamless sleep, nirvana
Is to be not this, not this.

A dying seabird standing where the burn runs to the shore
Between rank leaves and rough stone,
Its nictitating membrane down
Over eyes that knew a wild cold sky,
Head indrawn
Into neck-plumage and wing pinnae furled,
Disturbed in its dying becomes for the last time a gull,
Opens eyes on the world,
Brandishes harsh bill

And then withdraws again to live its death
And unbecome the gull-mask it was.

The dying are the initiates of mystery.
I have heard tell on lonely western shores
Of a light that travels the way the dead go by.
Upon an old door in his byre a MacKinnon saw it play
Where afterwards a dead man lay.
A MacIsaac watched it come over the sea
The way a young girl was rowed home from an isle.
It is a different light from ours, they say,
More beautiful.
They tell too of a darkness
That overwhelms and stifles flesh and blood
As the death-coach goes by,
For the living cannot travel by that invisible way;
But when a soul departs, a white bird flies:
Gull, gannet, tern or swan? Not these,
Another kind of bird
Into the emptiness untrammelled soars.

6

ONE night in a dream
The poet who had died a year ago
Led me up the ancient stair
Of an ancestral tower of stone.
Towards us out of the dark blew such sweet air
It was the warm breath of the spirit, I knew,
Fragrant with wild thyme that grew
In childhood's fields; he led me on,
Touched a thin partition, and was gone.
Beyond the fallen barrier
Bright over sweet meadows rose the sun.

THE WELL

THE poem I wrote was not the poem
That sang in my own voice
Out of the past a phrase of Gaelic song,
And with the song rose scent of birch, and birds
In skies long set, ancestral gloaming,
As love and grief rose up from the beginning
And joy from lives long gone,
And I knew all they and the song had known.

When I, a child who spoke with a northern tongue
Telling of a land of birch and heather,
Dipped my country dipper in a stone well,
Sand-grains danced where the spring rose so clear,
Its water seemed a place purer than air
I could not enter, though I dipped my hands in,
And saw my face reflected in its cold brim,
And filled my buckets and carried the water home.

The poem I wrote was not the poem that in a dream
Opened a well where water flowed again.
I cleared dead leaves away with my hand,
But inextricable weeds had grown
Rooted in the ancestral fountain;
And yet the water flowed
Pure from its inexhaustible hidden source,
And all to whom that water came . . .
In my dream I bathed a new-born child
And washed away the human stain.

An exile I have drunk from the Castalian spring,
But not such water as there rose.

THE PATH

I HAVE walked on waves of stone
Not knowing that the ground I trod
Is mirage in a watery glass,
A shimmering play of travelling light
Whose dangerous seas we call a world.
The shadow of the pleasure-dome
Midway floats, but deeper drown
All images on that surface cast.
Houses and cities seem and pass
On the meniscus of the flood.

There is a path over all waters
Leading to my feet alone
I have seen radiant from the sun
Setting beyond Skye and the more distant isles,
And rising over the rainbow seas of Greece.
It is the way to the sun's gate,
And I must walk that path of fire
That trembles, is scattered, reassembles
On all the sunlit moonlit waters of the world.

DREAM-FLOWERS

IN last night's dream who put into my hand
Two sprigs of verbena, culled from what sweet tree?
Your mother, it was told me, though I could not see her:
But to what daughter and by what mother,
By what Demeter to what Persephone given?
Was the hand mine that took those flowers
Given from one world to another?

There is a speech by none in this life spoken,
Yet we the speakers, we the listeners seem;
In that discourse, all signifies:
But what mind means the meaning that then is known?

Flowers of the earth grow out of the mystery;
From the deep loam of what has been
The past rises up in their life-stream
On whose surface images form and re-form;
But dreams rise up from a deeper spring:
Not from the past nor from the future come, but from the origin
These semblances of knowledge veiled in being.

THE REFLECTED LIGHT

YES I have seen the full moon climb from under yon black fell;
Golden orbed though tinged with blood and ashes she seemed
Since long ago immaculate gliding through these heavens
Coleridge with creation's eye watched moon's epiphany.

I too with world's vision have seen world rise and set,
All that light's shuttle weaves and night unweaves again
From astral spindles wound of moss and star I have loved,
And from my veins the constellations poured when my heart died.

Oh do not look with grief tonight at that dead moon
Or listen overmuch to the outcrying voices
The mourners and the weepers veiled and shrouded,
But let night bleed away all pain until the veins are dry
Of the rocks of the aged earth and ocean of ageless sky.

Moon of blood, you the last drop hang throbbing
Heavy like a tear with your full weight of sorrow:
Fall now, and flow away! You are a semblance
I and the world have seen too long; I'll change the theme
You from your orb reflect in creation's gazing glass,
Image imagined innumerable receding down distances
All bound for nothingness.
I'll turn away to seek the greater light.

And I was left gazing up into the heavens within
As some new joy in me took flight to its own place.

[123]

EILEANN CHANAIDH

For Margaret and John Lorne Campbell of Canna

1. The Ancient Speech

A GAELIC bard they praise who in fourteen adjectives
Named the one indivisible soul of his glen;
For what are the bens and the glens but manifold qualities,
Immeasurable complexities of soul?
What are these isles but a song sung by island voices?
The herdsman sings ancestral memories
And the song makes the singer wise,
But only while he sings
Songs that were old when the old themselves were young,
Songs of these hills only, and of no isles but these.
For other hills and isles this language has no words.

The mountains are like manna, for one day given,
To each his own:
Strangers have crossed the sound, but not the sound of the
      dark oarsmen
Or the golden-haired sons of kings,
Strangers whose thought is not formed to the cadence of
      waves,
Rhythm of the sickle, oar and milking-pail,
Whose words make loved things strange and small,
Emptied of all that made them heart-felt or bright.

Our words keep no faith with the soul of the world.

2. Highland Graveyard

TODAY a fine old face has gone under the soil;
For generations past women hereabouts have borne
Her same name and stamp of feature.
Her brief identity was not her own
But theirs who formed and sent her out

[124]

To wear the proud bones of her clan, and live its story,
Who now receive back into the ground
Worn features of ancestral mould.

A dry-stone wall bounds off the dislimned clay
Of many an old face forgotten and young face gone
From boundless nature, sea and sky.
A wind-withered escalonia like a song
Of ancient tenderness lives on
Some woman's living fingers set as shelter for the dead, to tell
In evergreen unwritten leaves,
In scent of leaves in western rain
That one remembered who is herself forgotten.

Many songs they knew who now are silent.
Into their memories the dead are gone
Who haunt the living in an ancient tongue
Sung by old voices to the young,
Telling of sea and isles, of boat and byre and glen;
And from their music the living are reborn
Into a remembered land,
To call ancestral memories home
And all that ancient grief and love our own.

3. The Island Cross

Memories few and deep-grained
Simple and certain mark this Celtic stone
Cross eroded by wind and rain.
All but effaced the hound, the horseman and the strange beast,
Yet clear in their signature the ancient soul
Where these were native as to their hunting-hill.

Against grain of granite
Hardness of crystalline rock-form mineral
Form spiritual is countergrained, against nature traced
Man's memories of Paradise and hope of Heaven.
More complex than Patrick's emblem green trifoliate
Patterning the tree soul's windings interlace
Intricate without end its labyrinth.

[125]

Their features wind-worn and rain-wasted the man and woman
Stand, their rude mere selves
Exposed to the summers and winters of a thousand years.
The god on the cross is man of the same rude race,
By the same hand made from the enduring stone;
And all the winds and waves have not effaced
The vision by Adam seen, those forms of wisdom
From memory of mankind ineffaceable.

4. Nameless Islets

Who dreams these isles,
Image bright in eyes
Of sea-birds circling rocky shores
Where waves beat upon rock, or rock-face smiles
Winter and summer, storm and fair?
In eyes of eider clear under ever-moving ripples the dart
  and tremor of life;
Bent-grass and wind-dried heather is a curlew's thought,
Gull gazes into being white and shell-strewn sands.

Joy harsh and strange traced in the dawn
A faint and far mirage; to souls archaic and cold
Sun-warmed stones and fish-giving sea were mother stern,
Stone omphalos, birth-caves dark, lost beyond recall.
Home is an image written in the soul,
To each its own: the new-born home to a memory,
Bird-souls, sea-souls, and with them bring anew
The isles that formed the souls, and souls the isles
Are ever building, shell by painted shell
And stone by glittering stone.
The isles are at rest in vision secret and wild,
And high the cliffs in eagle heart exult,
And warm the brown sea-wrack to the seals,
And lichened rocks grey in the buzzard's eye.

5. Stone on High Crag

Still stone
In heart of hill
Here alone
Hoodie and buzzard
By ways of air
Circling come.
From far shine
On wind-worn pinnacle
Star and moon
And sun, sun,
Wings bright in sun
Turn and return.

Centre of wing-spanned
Wheeling ways
Older than menhir
Lichen-roughened
Granite-grained
Rock-red
Rain-pocketed
Wind-buffeted
Heat-holding
Bird-whitened
Beak-worn
Insect-labyrinthine
Turf-embedded
Night-during
Race-remembered
Stand the known.

6. SHADOW

BECAUSE I see these mountains they are brought low,
Because I drink these waters they are bitter,
Because I tread these black rocks they are barren,
Because I have found these islands they are lost;
Upon seal and seabird dreaming their innocent world
My shadow has fallen.

THE HALT

For Dorothy Carrington

TRAVELLING in trains of time, succession and causality
From sleep to sleep, from dream to dream we pass,
Desire from day to day drawing us on
But never bringing to our abiding-place,
For with our exiled selves we everywhere remain.

A long and ruinous track with many tunnels –
Such was the symbol given, the aspect worn.
The trains still ran, but not to my destination:
In distance and in time I had reached a stand-still.
It seemed that time itself was being dismantled,
For as I watched, the iron tracks were gone.

I had not reached the place to which I travel
Nor any place; a halt on the long journey:
Yet to be out of those trains seemed freedom restored,
My own free-will, fragile as life of wren or grass-blade,
And where the iron way had been there was earth
And rock fresh fallen from a mountain-side,
And mountain air to breathe.

If all this may seem,
Summoned up by the magician of the dreaming mind,
Why so meagre, why such bare soil, sharp rock,
Why this place scarcely a place at all?

Could not the dream have brought the traveller home
To the high unchanging country beyond time,
Given back the spring, the tree, the singing bird?
But dreams tell truth: I am not there
But at that very place I seem to be.

MOVING IMAGE

INVIOLATE spaces from infinite centre created at the opening of
    an eye
World-wide into vision flow where on bright surfaces of light
The mountain isles rest in a dream whose radiant hemisphere
From zenith to horizon opens blue distances of sky and ocean
Which I alone of all created souls enjoy and am.
All around me in creatures that swim and dive and bask and fly
Spirit is at play in manifold multiform,
Each life in its own crystal sphere unbounded whose centre is
    primal joy.

Eighteen eider, three merganser, a jagged row of cormorant,
Gulls white as peace, ringed plover with thrilling cry
Wild over rotting weed and shells and fallen feathers play,
Upon the grey and orange-spreckled weed-brown sun-warmed
    wave-rounded rocks
Nine Atlantic seal I hear breathing in voices gruff
And voices clear melodious singing of weed and wave and sun.
Their brown and gray and orange-spreckled pelts are warm,
In them I feel the sun, in them slip without ripple into the
    glass-clear sea
Where in the heave of wave aurelia pulse with dim life
Unknown to the drifting tangle of algae green and red.
All abide in their unending now
Whose only labour is to be, to plunge and glide and soar.

Worlds within world each iridescent sphere of life revolves;
Its times and places are and pass like clouds over solitudes

As each grain of glistering quartz opens expanses great
    as mountains
And the Cuillin of Skye in light and shadow weightless as
    changing thought
In whose unfathomed heights and depths this ever-moving
    image and mirage.

THE ELEMENTALS

SAY I was where in dream I seemed to be
(Since seeming is a mode of being)
And by analogy say a curtain, veil or door,
A mist, a shadow, an image or a world was gone,
And other semblances behind appeared.
Perhaps a seeming behind the real those giant presences,
But seemed reality behind a seeming,
For they were fraught with power, beauty and awe:
The images before those meanings pale.

What seemed, then, was the world behind the world,
But just behind, and through the thinnest surface,
Not uncreated light nor deepest darkness,
But those abiding essences the rocks and hills and mountains
Are to themselves, and not to human sense.
Persons they appeared, but not personified;
Rather rock, hill and crag are aspects worn:
Shape-shifters they are, appear and disappear,
Protean assume their guises and transformations
Each in as many forms as eyes behold.

They received me neither as kindred nor as stranger,
Neither welcome nor unwelcome was I in their world;
But I, an exile from their state and station
Made from the place of meeting and parting where I stood, the sign
Signature and emblem of the human
Condition of conflict, anguish, love and pain and death and joy,

And they in harmony obeyed the Cross
Inscribed in the foundation of their world and mine.
From height to depth, circumference to centre
The primal ray, axis of world's darkness
Through all the planes of being descends into the prison of the rocks
Where elements in tumultuous voices wordless utter their wild *credo*.

THE EIGHTH SPHERE

THIS litel spot of erthe, that with the se embraced is
Priam's Troilus' light ghost beyond the moon ascending
son – of Troy Leaving within this sphere of space we call infinity
Those elements whose warring makes up life sublunary
destroyed Travelled in Scipio's track, who from a distant place,
Carthage in Clear and brilliant in the celestial heights, looked down,
Panic war And saw among the sempiternal stars and constellations
This low and heavy world, this rigid prison,
Small and far from heaven shining with borrowed light.

← Troilus on the forever shape-shifting surface,
Eliot With the beginning saw the end of his desire,
Fading flower of that immortal tree of stars.
Scipio saw Carthage there, how small a spot
Among those seas and continents, but blotting out all galaxies
When to the assault he came which razed from time
founder's Dido's bright palaces.
queen of Carthage

Dreams enlighten the living, dreamers from the dead learn wisdom:
Troilus dead and dreaming Scipio saw world as dream within dream.
The empirical doctor of souls, sleeping and waking
Between life and death watched the earth turning
Its cloudy globe of continent and ocean
While every sphere and star utters its own sound for ever.

Why then on earth? all ask who have been there,
Why in the body's narrow prison? They say

We are the appointed guardians of this globe, dreaming in its own spaces,
Nor without his command by whom the souls are sent must we depart;
We see the approaching body of our fate
And go to live each our appointed death, to die our life.
How could we from those heights look back on the undone, *forsaken T. for Diomedes*
Carthage not conquered or Criseydē unloved?
Earth's story must all be told, nothing left out.

St. Catherine I, like that other Cathie, wept in heaven
Until I was set down on a bare January northern moor,
Turned back from my ascent into the freedom of that sky
I ever since have longed to soar again.
But why this here and now only when I loved I knew,
And lifted up with joy the burden of this sorrow.

THE WILDERNESS

I CAME too late to the hills: they were swept bare
Winters before I was born of song and story,
Of spell or speech with power of oracle or invocation,

The great ash long dead by a roofless house, its branches rotten,
The voice of the crows an inarticulate cry,
And from the wells and springs the holy water ebbed away.

A child I ran in the wind on a withered moor
Crying out after those great presences who were not there,
Long lost in the forgetfulness of the forgotten.

Only the archaic forms themselves could tell
In sacred speech of hoodie on grey stone, or hawk in air,
sm. tree Of Eden where the lonely rowan bends over the dark pool.

Yet I have glimpsed the bright mountain behind the mountain,
Knowledge under the leaves, tasted the bitter berries red,
Drunk water cold and clear from an inexhaustible hidden fountain.

AS A CHILD FORGOTTEN . . .

For Herbert Read

As a child forgotten in a room filled with dusk
Sitting before a mute keyboard strikes one piano key
Then listens as the throbbing note diminishes and vanishes
And into silence passes with the sound,
So those who listen after with a longing that goes beyond
The dying away for ever of the most beautiful and dear
May follow the heard into the unheard, into the stillness
Of incorporeal mental spaces unbounded, the heavens
Whence and whither the fleeting music of the world is
    speeding.

THE STAR

I THOUGHT because I had looked into your eyes
And on our level eyebeams the world at rest
In motion turned upon its steady pole
That I had passed beyond the places and the times of sorrow.
My soul said to me, 'You have come home to here and now:
Before all worlds this beam of love began, and it runs on
And we and worlds are woven of its rays.'
But after I am in absence as before,
And my true love proved false as any other.
We looked away, and never looked again
Along the gaze that runs from love to love for ever:
So far? I wondered, looking at a star
Tonight above my house.

NINE ITALIAN POEMS

For Hubert and Lelia Howard

Natura Naturans

Veil upon veil
Petal and shell and scale
The dancer of the whirling dance lets fall.

Visible veils the invisible
Reveal, conceal
In bodies that most resemble
The fleeting mind of nature never still.

A young princess
Sealed in the perfect signature of what she was
With her grave lips of silent dust imparts a mystery
Hidden two thousand years under the Appian Way.

A frond in the coal,
An angel traced upon a crumbling wall,
Empty chrysalids of that bright ephemerid the soul.

Dea

Her marble hand proffers to all who pass
Ageless through time an ear of ripened corn
And with the corn a heavy head of poppy.
Her lips of stone impart a sacred silence
That some have understood and none may break.
She who is older than the rocks with her moon-silver sickle
These emblems culled of knowledge reaped, oblivion sown,
Behold, a mystery shows, though not to all.
The secret of the risen corn soul elsewhere remembers;
But here innumerable and small her scattered poppy-seed
Of moments, hours and days and months and years forgotten.
And after these was shown another sign, obscured by blood,
Partly human, more sorrowful to contemplate than these
Of life in death our pledge and gift from violated heaven.

IMAGES

AGAIN this morning trembles on the swift stream the image of the sun
Dimmed and pulsing shadow insubstantial of the bright one
That scatters innumerable as eyes these discs of light scaling the water.
From a dream foolish and sorrowful I return to this day's morning
And words are said as the thread slips away of a ravelled story:
'The new-born have forgotten that great burden of pain
World has endured before you came.'
A marble Eros sleeps in peace unbroken by the fountain
Out of what toils of ever-suffering love conceived?
Only the gods can bear our memories:
We in their lineaments serene
That look down on us with untroubled gaze
Fathom our own mind and what it is
Cleansed from the blood we shed, the deaths we die.

How many tears have traced those still unfading presences
Who on dim walls depict spirit's immortal joy?
They look from beyond time on sorrow upon sorrow of ours
And of our broken many our whole truth one angel tells,
Ingathers to its golden abiding form the light we scatter,
And winged with unconsuming fire our shattered image reassembles.
My load of memory is almost full;
But here and now I see once more mirrored the semblance of the
        radiant source
Whose image the fleet waters break but cannot bear away.

STATUES

THEY more than we are what we are,
Serenity and joy
We lost or never found,
The forms of heart's desire,
We gave them what we could not keep,
We made them what we cannot be.

Their kingdom is our dream, but who can say
If they or we

[135]

Are dream or dreamer, signet or clay;
If the most perfect be most true
These faces pure, these bodies poised in thought
Are substance of our form,
And we the confused shadows cast.

Growing towards their prime, they take our years away,
And from our deaths they rise
Immortal in the life we lose.
The gods consume us, but restore
More than we were:
We love, that they may be,
They are, that we may know.

OLD PAINTINGS ON ITALIAN WALLS

WHO could have thought that men and women could feel
With consciousness so delicate such tender secret joy?
With finger-tips of touch as fine as music
They greet one another on viols of painted gold
Attuned to harmonies of world with world.
They sense, with inward look and breath withheld,
The stir of invisible presences
Upon the threshold of the human heart alighting,
Angels winged with air, with transparent light,
Archangels with wings of fire and faces veiled.
Their eyes gleam with wisdom radiant from an invisible sun.

Others contemplate the mysteries of sorrow.
Some have carried the stigmata, themselves icons
Depicting a passion no man as man can know,
We being ignorant of what we do.
And painted wounded hands are by the same knowledge formed,
Beyond the ragged ache that flesh can bear
And we with blunted mind and senses dulled endure.
Giotto's compassionate eyes, rapt in sympathy of grief
See the soul's wounds that hate has given to love,

And those which love must bear
With the spirit that suffers always and everywhere.

Those painted shapes stilled in perpetual adoration
Behold in visible form invisible essences
That hold their gaze entranced through centuries; and we
In true miraculous icons may see still what they see
Though the saced lineaments grow faint, the outlines crumble
And the golden heavens grow dim
Where the Pantocrator shows in vain wounds once held precious.
Paint and stone will not hold them to our world
When those who once cast their bright shadows on these walls
Have faded from our ken, we from their knowledge fallen.

TRIAD

To those who speak to the many deaf ears attend.
To those who speak to one,
In poet's song and voice of bird,
Many listen; but the voice that speaks to none
By all is heard:
Sound of the wind, music of the stars, prophetic word.

DAISIES OF FLORENCE

BAMBINI picking daisies in the new spring grass
Of the Boboli gardens
Now and now and now in rosy-petalled fingers hold
The multitude of time.
To the limits of the small and fine florets innumerable of white
    and gold
They know their daisies real.

Botticelli with daisies from the timeless fields of recollection scatters
That bright Elysium or Paradise
Whose flowers none can gather,
Where spirits golden immortal walk for ever
With her who walks through spring after spring in primavera robed,
Ripening the transient under her veil.

The Eternal Child

A LITTLE child
Enters by a secret door, alone,
Was not, and is,
Carrying his torch aflame.

In pilgrim cloak and hood
Many and many come,
Or is it the one child
Again and again?

What journey do they go,
What quest accomplish, task fulfil?
Whence they cannot say,
Whither we cannot tell,
And yet the way they know.

So many innocents,
Reflections in a torrent thrown:
Can any on these treacherous waters cast,
Unmarred, unbroken,
Image the perfect one?

All things seem possible to the new-born;
But each one story tells, one dream
Leaves on the threshold of unbounded night
Where all return
Spent torch and pilgrim shroud.

Scala Coeli

WE do not see them come,
Their great wings furled, their boundless forms infolded
Smaller than poppy-seed or grain of corn
To enter the dimensions of our world,
In time to unfold what in eternity they are,
Each a great sun, but dwindled to a star
By the distances they have travelled.

Higher than cupola their bright ingress;
Presences vaster than the vault of night,
Incorporeal mental spaces infinite
Diminished to a point and to a moment brought
Through the everywhere and nowhere invisible door
By the many ways they know
The thoughts of wisdom pass.
In seed that drifts in air, or on the water's flow
They come to us down ages long as dreams
Or instantaneous as delight.

As from seed, tree flower and fruit
Grow and fade like a dissolving cloud,
Or as the impress of the wind
Makes waves and ripples spread,
They move unseen across our times and spaces.
We try to hold them, trace on walls
Of cave, cave-temple or monastic cell their shadows cast:
Animal-forms, warriors, dancers, winged angels, words of power
On precious leaves inscribed in gold or lapis lazuli,
Or arabesques in likeness of the ever-flowing.

They show us gardens of Paradise, holy mountains
Where water of life springs from rock or lion's mouth,
Walk with us unseen, put into our hands emblems,
An ear of corn, pine-cone, lotus, looking-glass or chalice;
As dolphin, peacock, hare or moth or serpent show themselves,
Or human-formed, a veiled bride, a boy bearing a torch,
Shrouded or robed or crowned, four-faced,
Sounding lyre or sistrum, or crying in bird-voices;
Water and dust and light
Reflect their images as they slowly come and swiftly pass.

We do not see them go
From visible into invisible like gossamer in the sun.
Bodies by spirit raised
Fall as dust to dust when the wind drops,
Moth-wing and chrysalis.
Those who live us and outlive us do not stay,

But leave empty their semblances, icons, bodies
Of long-enduring gold, or the fleet golden flower
On which the Buddha smiled.
In vain we look for them where others found them,
For by the vanishing stair of time immortals are for ever departing;
But while we gaze after the receding vision
Others are already descending through gates of ivory and horn.

LAST THINGS

1

I PAUSED in a garden-alley of cypress and rose, resembling Paradise;
But I had come as a stranger to that place
And my thought was (and already it is so)
'This garden will be as other gardens gone
Where I have said, here let me stay.'
For now and now and now moves on
Though none perceives the present come or go
Carrying bird from sheltering tree more swiftly than wings.

The self in exile is the wandering mind
Travelling without rest through times and places.
We cannot lengthen the conscious moment by one heart-beat,
Sense-bound travel the great sphere where all is present,
Paradise, lost to us, that very place we are,
Outcast beneath the tree whose fruits we gather.

There is a mind whose here is everywhere, whose now all time;
And sometimes we know with its knowledge, in dream or waking;
Is that mind ours, veiled by continual forgetting,
Are we its thoughts astray?
The old, whose souls like ripened seed after the fall of flower
Shake loose from body to be sown anew or harvested,
Seem at times to be present in past presents
As a shell held to the ear carries the sound of waves

Breaking on distant sands still wet from an ebbing tide.
And I already in early morning sometimes wake
Upon the threshold of some long past day;
A tree stands on the brink of light
White with blossoms as once beside a house long desolate.

It is said that body is soul's sepulchre
From whose sleep of oblivion the dead shall rise,
Consciousness from enshrouding flesh and blood stripped bare;
'For is not memory that dread Book of Judgment,'
The poet with the Sibyl testifies,
In whose pages indelible all is written?
What sanctuary, what labyrinthine garden then shall hide
Self from self-knowledge, self-condemned?
We are ourselves those regions we must inherit,
The places of our sorrow await us in our past
Where like the opium-eater we must dream
Back down the long corridors of time,
In vanished cities walking with the dead.

Some have with Blake and with the visionary of Patmos cried
'Come,' desiring only that day's glory,
When the last blade of grass and particle of dust shall rise
Out of the past to be for ever what it is,
Each in its own time and place within the abiding sphere.
Remembrance to the just is Paradise regained,
And not one sparrow fallen
Or leaf or star shaken from the abundant tree.
But who, knowing the end with the beginning
Of earth's dust and ashes, and love betrayed,
Shall not wake with a cry at all man must remember?

2

ALL is judged,
The shadow by the leaf,
Flower by star,
The great tree by its seed.
The perfect is not in time

Where all is marred;
But lucid forms
Cast their images
Upon our waters:
Their faces, veiled or radiant, are always beautiful,
For we imagine them,
They are the aspects of our wisdom.
They bring us messages, intellections,
Impart a mystery,
Could tell us more, if we could hold their gaze.

They play on delicate instruments of joy,
Or cry in harmony the chord of creation,
Tone and overtone,
And when their trumpets sound
The doom of the world is a great music
Wrecking our images on its waves.
From regions of mind forgotten,
The frontiers of our consciousness invading
The Pantocrator raises no hand of power
When all is judged,
The shadow by the real
Being in recollection what it is,
We what we are.

SOLILOQUIES UPON LOVE

1

To realise of the all one possibility
(Whose one could not be all without our many)
A life to live, beginning, middle and ending,
Each chooses (so it was told by one who came back from the dead)
Knowing how it will be; and choice is fate.
Others have told that we shall see the pattern hereafter,
Know the causes and meaning of what now we endure and are.
Some choose from folly and some from wisdom a state of being;

Yet, folly or wisdom, something to be compassed,
In stress and tension held upon the slowly-turning ever-changing surface
Of a spinning filmy bubble-world of dreams enacted:
The wanderer that home-coming he always travelled towards,
And Orpheus his lonely soaring strong white wings.
Need I then so much care
Whether in sorrow or in joy I fathom the mind in whose infinite reaches
I am not the knower but the known, the imagined?

All is one in that sphere whose times are lives,
Whose places that inexhaustible knowledge we call a world;
But world to us is full of distances:
We measure near and far from our sole desire,
Blood heart or spirit's hope and longing and despair.
Who but we could dream such heights and depths of separation?
Like planets drifted astray from sun or nebula we travel
Away and away into the empty night
Whose end we do not know, but only its duration.

Dante knew love as immeasurable absence
And turned from the world to find elsewhere a presence
Where after time-long Purgatory dawns the eternal light.
He in that soul who gazed upon his soul
Beheld the aspect and the vehicle of wisdom
Which lay beyond, farther than he had come.
Keats laid upon a warm and bodily breast his star of life,
Yet beauty's shadow touched his lips in death,
Endymion's kiss the recompense
Of an immortal to a burning mortal love consumed
To dust and ashes in a consecrated urn.

It is my lot to watch the receding of a star
Whose sole light a great darkness first made known.
I am a point whose line is cast so far
From there to here, from then to now
That I can tell of love's outer spaces,
And of a stillness that upholds
All who come there, and seem to fall no more,
But learn that as love's light, so is its darkness.

THERE is a pattern, a design beaten in metal, carved in stone,
Danced on the dancing-floor, leading down into the tomb,
From ancient Crete travelling all human ways by land and sea;
More treasured than fine gold of cup or breast-plate that
      inscribed form
Not to be found in nature, revealed to mind alone,
An intellection hammered in bright gold.
Involving and evolving helices meet at a point and part,
Periphery to centre, centre to spiral widening they run
While Ariadne still for Theseus holds the thread.

Descent, return; sleep, waking; darkness, light:
A thousand years they journey, so Plato fables,
From death to birth who crave the gift of life,
And with each sole desire slow time keeps faith:
Certain the hour of love as the hour of death,
Fate at the centre waits where the clue runs out.

Knowledge beyond joy and grief that confrontation in the heart
      of the heart's maze;
I say, for this I came, loss, absence and this sorrow.
I have gained my loss; gained at the price of loss
Epiphany of love, alike to joy and sorrow ever-present;
By mourning known: blessed are they that mourn.
Many have travelled the long winding way for less.

Destiny is but one,
And when it is accomplished, all is done.
Is this dark centre end or beginning of the way I have come?

3

THEY pass unnoticed, the moulded lips of the goddess, the athlete's
    stance,
The grace of the shoe-shine *kouroi* everyone drives away.
Young Athenians at a café table gesturing with nimble wrists
Have those full pencilled eyes, those profiles, lacking only the beard
    of Odysseus,

Painters of amphorae depicted three thousand years ago, that beauty
    of race.
A paper towel handed with archaic gesture of sculptured *choephorae*
Bearing upon open palms an offering to the gods; the great hurl of
    Poseidon
Obscured in cement-dust; a beggar-girl walking like a caryatid
Alone in her misery as banished Electra,
Lingers in her exile at the 'bus terminus for Chalchis, where
    Agamemnon's other daughter was sacrificed.
They sell indifferent skills for menial wages, whose beauty was once
    beyond price,
Themselves least of all knowing what in such fleeting forms old
    sculptors saw:
Our age has other values.

The Venus of the Cyclades has no face; the crude act she celebrates
Requires none: those simple ancestors prized the *mons veneris*, not the
    eyes or braided hair.
Yet something stood apart from the act of lust, to depict a triangle, a shell,
A megalith at once phallus and man with eyes and sword: the essentials.
Such simple aspects are yet human; knowledge begins in wonder,
And imagination first gave to the crude genitals divine *mana*
Before love could endure to stand apart and contemplate entire
Perfection of embodied soul, man, woman, lion, sea-horse, ideas of
    beauty.
Body's unopened eyes never could see that young charioteer
So lightly holding the reins, composed, centred in his own solitude,
    remote;
Nor the wind-flower *kore* on her tomb who with inverted torch is
    departing
With the psychopompos whose ankle-bones are winged for flight from
    world to world.
Soul journeys from body into its own perfection
As pure the moon rides clear of dissolving shadow of shapeless cloud.

Love, blind to imperfection, sees only the perfect;
But from how great a distance the inviolate casts its images
Whose gleams upon our waters ignorance plunges after;
To body a seeming that is not, whose being eludes passion's embrace.

No-one has possessed beauty: how can we from an intellection dream
    of requited love?
It is we who are possessed, drawn beyond earth's downward pull of
    flesh and blood
Into another sphere: beauty confers the gift of exile.

4

Not hand in hand; I take that solitary way alone
From the isle of orcs and seals and sea-mew's clang;
But meeting, long after, in a city street, my dear companion,
It was as if the grave had opened and the light shone in.
I thought the resurrection-day had come,
For as we stood together, all sorrow was gone.
Sorrow remembers joy, but joy is beyond time soul's nature;
Crystal spaces opened about us,
Over blue glittering seas the wheeling tern and soaring gulls, so often
    seen,
On the wet sand the plover ran on rapid feet among shining shells,
And from the bay voices of eider floating at peace.
On the budding alder by the burn the green linnet sang,
The yellow iris bloomed, and rowan white and green
As once before our eyes; were these the same?
In that remembered world, had body ever been,
Or had we, thinking we were on bodily ground, walked in the eternal
    mind?
Together, as once there, we forgot that Paradise was lost,
Whose times and places, in the world we travelled now, no longer were.
In that moment out of time all was as it had been;
Innocence did not seem strange to us, but our simple selves.
Then on those infinite skies and seas of light, and living voices,
The grave closed again,
As if earthquake had made Hades' prison gape, then shut its chasm.
Back among shadows I turned and walked away from the brightness
Where once in flesh and blood I was here and now in my love's house.
In time all is departure: body can never return.
With what but memory can soul keep faith that what was, is, and is to
    come?

5

YOUR gift to me was a grey stone cast upon a wild shore, traced over
With calligraphy of inscrutable life. A marine annelid
With stroke as free as by master-brush, one fluent word
Has written with its life in the record of the *logos*,
Yet lacked senses to see its delicate coils and meanders of white masonry.
Mind unknown that blind plasm signed
With weight and drift of sea, of wave-refracted light, and stress of spirit
Omnipresent in every part, universal being here imprinted.
The number-loving Greeks built their white temples
To Apollo of the measured and Aphrodite the veiled source:
Does the same harmony inform those marble shells,
The word that is and means always and everywhere the same?
Your message of life to life was written on the sea-floor before we were;
Serpentine, strange and clear
The deep knowledge we share, who are not the knowers but the known.
You gave and I received as beauty what the *logos* writes:
Intelligible, though not to us, the inscription on the stone.

THE seas go dry, the rocks melt in the sun:
These things come to pass, and the sands run
As the unknown becomes the undone.

Against immeasurable nothing stands the *fiat*
Of sun and the other stars, and the unfolding rose:
One point of light puts back all darkness.

There all is transparent, light runs through light,
Each mirrored in every other, all see themselves in all,
Every star is all stars and the sun, the small is great,
There none walks upon alien soil;
From far we look into that heaven by the lifting of the head.

Melody there is played in tune, the rose unfading,
Earth and all seas the heavenly content of those heavens,
The gods traverse that country and that space at peace.
There too is my love's eternal dwelling:
Too long I have wept; I will go to my own place.

FROM

The Lost Country

(1971)

A HOUSE OF MUSIC

For Margaret Fay Shaw Campbell

SOUND of music in the house,
Stir of intangible shapes that pass
Tracing in the awakened air
Meanders of melodious flow,
Waves that ripple on their course,
Meet and mingle, melt and part.

Those graceful forms your fingers rouse
Move like figures in a glass,
Dancing shapes that come and go
Purified in that silver pool,
Elusive of enamoured sense,
Yet mix and mingle with our thought;
And through our still reflections glide
Boucher's or Watteau's vanished France,
Treading in a *fête champêtre*
A measure in an April wood,
Dancers who are not flesh and blood
But spirits of harpsichord and flute.
Still in their own world they move
To Couperin's or to Rameau's skill.

Shakespeare's King Richard in his prison
Could not check the disordered tune
Of the sour discordant world;
But heard with the true inward ear
A concord that could mend his state,
Sweeten the music of men's lives
And bring his kingdom under rule.
Pythagoras could charm and lull
An ignorant homicidal rage
Awake the powers of the soul
To modulated harmonies

Our noise and violence drown and dull,
But still in nature's octave play.

The earth of Eden, I have read,
In some old wise forgotten page,
Is sound; and trees of Paradise
The woven music of that chord
Sung by the morning choir of stars;
Complexities that ebb and flow
From original concord grow
Texture perceptible to sense.
Let but once that music cease
Or discord mar those subtle forms,
Eden is a wilderness,
The starry spaces barren ground.

Harmonious voices in the wind
Mould to their sound the listening ear,
Spirals that twine and intertwine
Tremble in the sensitive air
Till passive earth their imprint takes
And listens with an ear of clay
To that one Word the spirit speaks.

Caliban in his sleep could hear
Those island voices in a dream,
As all who listen are attuned
To shapes invisible but near,
Men who rock upon the tide
Whose lift and fall their impress bears,
Or women at the close of day
Attentive to the blackbird's note
Or wild sweet voices on the shore.

LETTER TO PIERRE EMMANUEL

'C'est que l'âme française, qui habite même les plus déracinés, est une des grands modes de l'intelligence et de la sensibilité humaines, indissolublement.' (Pierre Emmanuel, on his election to the Académie Française, 1969.)

'FRANCE, one of the great modes of the human mind and heart,
Indissolubly', you have declared; for the souls of nations, as of men,
Abide in that Yonder beyond time on whose frontiers we stray,
Looking for door or gate or breach in the wall, to enter, perhaps to return,
(Paris – so many portals into green retreats and spacious chambers,
Expressive modes of subtle feeling and fine thought
Where we may sometimes find, or seem to find, that place),
But the life, as of a man, so of a city
(Near the Invalides a garden-hose dripping perpetual spray
On grass and philadelphus, where children play with sand,
Artist and poet with images, in the quiet shade)
Corruptible, soluble in time's flow.
'Paris,' I too said on a June day in nineteen sixty-nine,
'Never from the beginning of the world to the end of time
Has been or will be so great a city dreamed by man.'

To be a barbarian is to have no past;
For the past is the present of the future, the human kingdom;
Some known to us, others unknown, you, I, that still continuing few
To whose hearts the remembered and forgotten dead are presences,
Ripening in memory the seed of cities
To scatter for what meagre crop this poisoned stricken earth may bear,
Or harvest into that native land we desire and remember,
Keep France, keep Christendom, keep Athens in mind.

Here at Royaumont a plaster gothic angel on the stair,
Image of an image, points with slender finger to a delicate half-forgotten
    heaven
To us who in a present far from that presence come and go
While the sun of yet one more summer
Opens centifoliate roses on the still standing wall
Of this reason-ruined house of God raised by the genius and the kings of
    France
Whose sanctuary the first shock of the Terror to come, laid low.

[153]

NINFA REVISITED

For Hubert and Lelia Howard

I, THE last poet it may be,
Of all the many there have been
To praise this ancient fertile place,
To walk beside such crystal streams
As water Dante's Paradise
And irrigate Boccaccio's shades,
Spenser's and Milton's bower of bliss,
Anemone and violet
Of Circe's or of Shelley's isles,
Here meet the remembered dead
For kinship or for poetry's sake
Nobility's invited guests
Under these green and blossoming boughs.
In my lifetime some I knew –
Eliot with sober mein,
Edwin Muir with gentle face,
Question if I fulfil my task;
Isak Dinesen, whose mask
These lilies gilded, 'Do you make
The puppet-master's meaning clear?'
Helen Sutherland, who claimed
From each according to our art –
It was her friendship brought me here.

At the Duchessa's desk I write,
Absent since five years ago,
And wonder if my words would please
The attentive and discerning ear
Of Marguerite Caetani, friend
Of St. John Perse and Valéry.
My hostess tends centennial trees,
Her only privilege her task,
To recreate felicity,
This ancient garden, ever new,
That some have found, and all desire,

And all believe on earth, somewhere,
Though none knows where, these flowers bloom,
In Persia, India, Avalon,
Whose multitude seems infinite:
Her art to make that legend true.

The rabble clamouring at the gates
Raise slogans of a future age;
They will break in, yet never find
Lost Eden, but the accursed ground
Of those who live by bread alone,
The thorns and thistles of the waste.
Rose and cypress are the dream
Of Adam awake in Paradise,
And fade into the common day:
No social justice can confer
Beauty's immeasurable gift,
Or touch with silent, secret joy
The crowds that envy and destroy.

Makers who neither toil nor spin
Labour to prolong that dream,
Their only task to recollect
Originals laid up in Heaven;
Every seed repeats its form,
Paradigm of leaf and tree,
And bees their secret honey find.
The toilers and the spinners build
A far other world than this.

In Paradise each man is born:
The orient wheatfields of Traherne
Fired by Blake's angel-peopled sun,
Wordsworth's tree, of many one:
Eden is for each alone
To cultivate, like old Voltaire,
Form in similitude of Heaven,
Or sell for money, or lay waste.
Proust's hawthorn-hedge was like another,

And Monet's drifting nenuphars
But for the dreams reflected there,
And Botticelli's *rose celeste*
Much like the common briar rose
Of the hedges those lay waste
Who serve the nihil of the age
And spray with weed-killer the flowers
Patterned upon Venus' dress.
It is the nightingale who sings
In her green oratory alone:
Who will attend so small a voice
Above the mechanistic noise?
The nightingale is but a word
In the lost speech of Paradise.

Civilisation has a price
Those know only who have paid.
Rome fought, in civilisation's cause,
Before the years of Christian grace
The barbarous nations at the gates
To keep that rabble horde at bay.
Rome declined; again there fails
A civilisation or a world,
And what is vanishing, I praise.

All that is high the gods have raised,
Agents of immortal life
Of beauty, wisdom, power and joy,
The four ever-established thrones
Poet, lover, scholar, ruler serve,
And on their linked chain of gold
Invisible, suspend a world
That else must fall into the void,
Beautyless, meaningless, profane.

A PAINTING BY WINIFRED NICHOLSON

SUNLIT green of a late summer hayfield
(The pikes all led and their faint circles faded)
Sheltered by abundant beech, goldening to autumn fire,
And beyond, soft English hills that close the view.
Some happy hand has gathered cistus, bergamot, scabious
From the untidy sheltered brick-walled border,
Taken a jug from the flower-room, and put them, just as they were,
(Giving them a little shake to free their plumage)
By the window, where a passing bee or butterfly may come.

'That is an old picture,' my friend said;
And I, 'How like the real world you and I remember.'
– For those same peaceful fields of vanished summer
Were spread alike for ladies of the castle
And for the niece of the village schoolteacher.

Fields, it is true, in the aftermath are still green,
Beeches turn brown, country flowers in unheeded gardens grow.
It is something else, we said, that will not come again,
That leisure, that ease of heart unsevered from its roots;
The things we thought about, some sweetness in the air, nuance
Of educated English speech, libraries, country lanes;
Few cars; 'wireless' a cat's whisker and a piece of quartz
Boys fiddled with. But there was laughter,
Songs at the piano, the Golden Bough, the Spirit of Man;
Pressed flowers; how fondly we took civilisation for granted!

CHILDHOOD

I SEE all, am all, all.
I leap along the line of the horizon hill,
I am a cloud in the high sky,
I trace the veins of intricate fern.
In the dark ivy wall the wren's world

Soft to bird breast nest of round eggs is mine,
Mine in the rowan tree, the blackbird's thought
Inviolate in leaves ensphered.
I am bird-world, leaf-life, I am wasp-world hung
Under low berry-branch of hidden thorn,
Friable paper-world humming with hate,
Moss-thought, rain-thought, stone still thought on the hill.

Never, never, never will I go home to be a child.

BY THE RIVER EDEN

1

NEVER twice that river
Though the still turning water
In its dark pools
Mirrors suspended green
Of an unchanging scene.

Frail bubbles revolve,
Break in the rippling falls,
The same, I could believe,
Each with its moment gone,
I watched in former years,

Ever-reforming maze
Of evening midge's dance,
Swifts that chase and scream
Touching in their low flight
The picture on the stream.

Heart is deceived,
Or knows what mind ignores:
Not the mirroring flux
Nor mirrored scene remain
Nor the rocky bed
Of the river's course,

But shadows intangible
That fade and come again.
Through their enduring forms
The glassy river runs;
All flows save the image
Cast on that shimmering screen.

2

BESIDE the river Eden
Some child has made her secret garden
On an alder strand
Marked out with pebbles in the sand,
Patterned with meadow flowers,
As once I did, and was.

My mother who from time past
Recalls the red spots on the yellow mimulus
That nodded in the burn
To her alone
Was that same child,

And hers, bedridden,
Mused on an old cracked darkened picture of a
        salmon-river
Painted in Paradise so long ago
None living ever saw those tumbling waters flow.
By her imagination made miraculous
Water of life poured over its faded varnished stones.

All is one, I or another,
She was I, she was my mother,
The same child for ever
Building the same green bower by the same river.

THE lapwing's wavering flight
Warns me from her nest,
Her wild sanctuary;
Dark wings, white breast.
The Nine Nicks have weathered,
Lichened slabs tumbled,
In sand under roots of thyme
Bone and feather lie,
The ceaseless wind has blown;
But over my grey head
The plover's unageing cry.

HEIRLOOM

SHE gave me childhood's flowers,
Heather and wild thyme,
Eyebright and tormentil,
Lichen's mealy cup
Dry on wind-scored stone,
The corbies on the rock,
The rowan by the burn.

Sea-marvels a child beheld
Out in the fisherman's boat,
Fringed pulsing violet
Medusa, sea-gooseberries,
Starfish on the sea-floor,
Cowries and rainbow-shells
From pools on a rocky shore,

Gave me her memories,
But kept her last treasure:
'When I was a lass,' she said,
'Sitting among the heather,
Suddenly I saw

That all the moor was alive!
I have told no-one before.'

That was my mother's tale.
Seventy years had gone
Since she saw the living skein
Of which the world is woven,
And having seen, knew all;
Through long indifferent years
Treasuring the priceless pearl.

SEEN FROM THE WINDOW OF
A RAILWAY-CARRIAGE

THEY arise, approach, majestic shapes, their aspects change,
    and pass,
Each mountain a memory the slow hills rise,
Pure forms of light, divine body in repose,
In frowning stone of northern corries rifts of snow,
Summits of peace of the alone with the alone
Approach majestic, turn in grandeur, slowly go.

Green bosom of the hills my childhood knew,
Grass of Parnassus, golden asphodel –
But I cannot leave the speeding train that carries me on
Into an older land where memories not mine
Of ancestors long dead lift to their hills mine eyes
As they approach majestic, turn in grandeur, change and pass.

My mother a life far other than Scotland's songs and stories tell
Lived in an alien place among trivial things
Disdaining to behold what was not of the dream
Of tenderness and pride her ancestors lived by
Till the misty shapes grew dim in memory
That now again in grandeur in their abiding places rise.

I would give back to the host whose lost world I inherit,
Rising from shrouded hearts, their longed-for land,
To my mother her girlhood's high heather moor,
To hers, the ferny linn, to my grandfather his salmon-river,
The substance of their dream, the wanting of their woe
Whose multitude in me clamours for their own
Ancestral hills that turn majestic their sunlit faces of enduring
      stone.

APRIL'S NEW APPLE BUDS ...

April's new apple buds on an old lichened tree;
Slender shadows quiver, celandines burn in the orchard grass –
This moment's image: how long does a moment stay?
I took, and look away, and look again, and see
The morning light has changed a little, the linnet flown; but who
      can say
When one moment's present became the next moment's past
To which this now was still the yet-to-be?
It seems, in this old walled garden, time does not pass,
Only mind wanders and returns; I watch attentively
And see not one green blade move out of its place.
The Easter daffodils, the shadows and the apple-trees
Phrases in music continuous from first to last.
To be is to be always here and now.
The green linnet flits from bough to bough.

I FELT UNDER MY OLD BREASTS ...

I felt, under my old breasts, this April day,
Young breasts, like leaf and flower to come, under grey apple-buds
And heard a young girl within me say,

'Let me be free of this winter bark, this toil-worn body,
I who am young,
My form subtle as a dream.'
And I replied, 'You, who are I,
Entered a sad house when you put on my clay.
This shabby menial self, and life-long time,
Bear with as you may
Until your ripening joy
Put off the dust and ashes that I am,
Like winter scales cast from the living tree.'

'THERE SHALL BE NO MORE SEA'

THESE rolling flowing plunging breaking everlasting weaving waters
Moved by tumultuous invisible currents of the air
Seem liquid light, seem flaming sun-ocean pouring fire,
And the heavy streaming windbeaten waves
Consubstantial with glint and gold-dazzle flashed from glassy crests.
On turbulence of light we float.

Why then should I not walk on water? Through water-walls
Of intangible light, mirage through mirage pass?
This body solid and visible to sense
Insubstantial as the shouting host of the changeable wind
Or fluent forms that plunge under wave, embrace passing through
    embrace,
Melting merging parting for ever,
Or oreads slender as a line of shadow moving across mountain's
    roseate face.

OREADS

No, our kind cannot live with these
Solitudes, desolations, steeps and distances –
Mere emptiness to us the great spaces, where at ease
Mountains repose; they make nothing of us.
Their being is not of our mode or scale.

Some see a man's face on a crag, but it is not so;
Yet rock has a face that we see sometimes smile
And sometimes close. Five Sisters of Kintail –
But no kindred of ours
Those sisters of wind and gale.

Veering beneath crests of snow
Only wings know
The wind and know its flow; eagle and crow
In air unbounded come and go.
Like ant on lichened stone the dun stag pastures on the
      moor below.

But shepherd under hill in hovel of stone
Living companionable with crag and storm
May hear them speak, the alone to the alone,
Beyond the compass of the known.
Pipe music has the sound of distance in its drone.

Or a child may stray
Away on the wild hills as far as eye can see
Whose sight unhindered runs where summit meets the sky.
In the lens of a buzzard's eye the hills lie.

So lost,
Into how vast a loneliness we are gathered,
Into a strangeness how remote,
Existence without end; presences that yet
Protect us from invading night
And the unbroken silence of the dead.

ON AN ANCIENT ISLE

So like, they seem the same,
The young shoots of the yellow iris sheathed leaf through leaf,
Lit green of glittering blades and shadows quivering on the sanded turf
Where limpet shells are strewn among the celandine
And driftwood from the surf.
So like they seem, almost I to my own memories had come home.

Never green leaf nor golden flower again;
Yet from the one immaculate root spring after spring
Upon this farthest Western shore the one Paradise,
Earth, sea and sky patterned with the one dream.
Traced on the wild that legendary land
More ancient than song or story or carved stone
My mother and her mother's mother knew: the green ways,
Clear wells, stones of power, presences
In hoodie's shape, high distant summits, hosts in the wind.
Signs in a language more heartfelt than holy book, or rune,
Each hill and hollow, each moving wing or shadow, means.
'Memory pours through the womb and lives in the air,'
And childhood with new eyes sees the for ever known:
The words by heart, we live the story as we will.

As I came over the hill to an unvisited shore
I seemed, though old, at the untold beginning of a familiar tale.

IN ANSWER TO A LETTER ASKING ME
FOR VOLUMES OF MY EARLY POEMS

You ask for those poems of Paradise
I wrote in heart's blood for your sake,
Yet this, your ultimate request,
Is made to me in bitterness.

If hate were love, if love were hate
It could not make our tale untold,
It could not make that blood unshed.
Yours and mine, all life's one stream,
One sole desire runs though our veins,
And each has done and suffered all
The passionate unending wrong
That spills the river all must wade
Who cross into that green, green land.

You ask me now, ten years gone by,
What I can bring you from past days,
What charm to solve the grief of life,
Or talisman of alchemic gold
To heal mortality? What use
My offering of woman's tears?
We have but so much in our veins
Of heart's red blood, not less, nor more
Than expiates the crime of birth,
Not more, nor less, than pays the price
Of our return to Paradise.

But if I were to tell you, 'There
The price we pay, the tears we shed,
The death all suffer, all forget',
(Those of that country cannot lie,
And yet, in this, the truth we tell
Few believe, and many hate)
If I should say, 'there at your door
The unheeded yellow iris blooms
Where rises the unending flow
Of living light's unsullied streams,
All stands in two worlds, and the ground
Of Paradise is everywhere,'
You would reply, 'Those mock despair
Who paint such pictures for the blind.'

The only Paradise, Proust said,
Is the lost country that has passed

Out of time and into mind,
Nor can we come into our own
Till time's last heart-beat has been sped,
Our sole desire all we have lost.
Plato, that we come from thence,
Out of mind and into time,
In a forgetful sleep descend,
And by remembering return
Where memory and hope are one,
The locked gate and the flaming sword
Intangible as a troubled dream.

But all we know is hearsay, save
The record in the Book of Life:
Where Sandaig burn runs to the shore,
Where tern and eider nest secure
On their far island salt and bare
Beyond our world of guilt and time,
Yonder I have seen you stand,
Innocent of all you bear:
What can I say but 'You are there,
And I, and all, did we but know,
Who weep and mourn in exile here.'

JUDAS-TREE

WHEN first I heard that story it seemed incredible
That one betrayed;
But now, having lived my own, more wonderful
That eleven stayed
Even so precariously, so stupidly, so tentatively faithful.
So few are true; and I,
In others as in myself despising him who died,
Not once but many times have done what Judas did,
Yet sorrowed less than he,
For I still live, not hang on any purple-blossoming tree.

MESSAGE TO GAVIN

Leaving you, I have come to Iona's strand
Where the far is near, and the dear, far.
Ardnamurchan's sea-dragon that guarded our south
Now bars the north with its stony jaw;
Staffa a barren rock across the sound
That seemed a mirage shimmering from some unreal land.

Eigg, Rhum and the Cuillin faded to a thin veil;
My eyes retrace the lines of long familiar hills
To find you beyond that texture of dream.
Absence is too hard for the remembering heart to learn –
I walk on your most distant shore:
One horizon enrings us still.

A dazzle of light on your sun's ocean path,
A hidden rock where the white surf foams,
The faintest feather of cloud in your sky –
Since not again can I be with you life with life
I would be with you as star with distant star,
As drop of water in the one bright bitter sea.

THE DEAD

Not because they are far, but because so near
The dead seem strange to us:
Stripped of those unprized familiar forms they wore,
Defending from our power to wound
That poignant naked thing they were,
The holy souls
Speak, essence to essence, heart to heart.
Scarcely can we dare
To know in such intimacy
Those whom courtesy, or reticence, or fear
Hid, when, covered in skins of beasts,

Evading and evaded,
We turned the faces of our souls away.
Only the youngest child is as near as they,
Or those who share the marriage-bed
When pity and tenderness dwell there.

FALLING LEAVES

Whirled dust, world dust,
Tossed and torn from trees,
No more they labour for life, no more
Shelter of green glade, shade
Of apples under leaf, lifted in air
They soar, no longer leaves.

What, wind that bears me,
Am I about to be? Will water
Draw me down among its multitude?
Earth shall I return, shall I return to the tree?
Or by fire go further
From myself than now I can know or dare?

LONG AGO I THOUGHT YOU YOUNG . . .

Long ago I thought you young, bright daimon,
Whisperer in my ear
Of springs of water, leaves and song of birds
By all time younger
Than I, who from the day of my conception
Began to age into experience and pain;
But now life in its cycle swings out of time again
I see how old you were,
Older by eternity than I, who, my hair grey,

Eyes dim with reading books,
Can never fathom those grave deep memories
Whose messenger you are,
Day-spring to the young, and to the old, ancient of days.

DREAMS

ONCE UPON EARTH THEY STOOD ...

ONCE upon earth they stood,
Tree and miraculous bird,
Water from holy well,
Lamp whose undying flame
Burns on within the tomb.

From grotto grove and shrine
Saints from their icons fade,
Their presences withdrawn;
Meanings from words are dead,
The springs gone under the hill.

Inviolate in dream
The mysteries still are shown,
The dead are living still;
But bring them back none may
Who wakes into this day.

HOMAGE TO C.G. JUNG

SANCTUARY that cannot be profaned, inviolate,
Intangible thought-forms come and go at will,
But not our will: in dream we must abide
The terrible and the beautiful, not there to be gainsaid,
What pleases the guisers to display, perforce attend,
Whose forms are meanings enigmatical
As oracles written on leaves scattered in the wind.

Not to be gainsaid: pursuer and pursued are cast
Uncomprehending into bliss or horror; tired in illusion
Struggle from act to act of phantasmagoria.
Truth is the language of that world, rambling in idiot's tale,
Or clear as the voice that chants the liturgy.
The hells too are holy, being truth: they are our own,
According to our condition the nightmare lies in wait.

Dreamers on ways most strange,
In prisons and churches, kings and murderers,
We meet our many selves, on grandiose quests,
Deep in guilt, touched by the hand of glory,
Flee our accusers into the common day
Or return, gifted with treasures from hidden treasuries
Of the great fallen kingdom lost under lidded night.

And sometimes in those fields, domains and gardens of light,
Native Paradise of whose birthright each possesses all,
Like knowledge, without diminution of the whole,
In every myriad mirror perfect the whole sun.
'A native of that happy country,' how have I strayed
Into works and days meaningless and profane?
Not far the way, though lost: many a night I have passed the
    guarded gate.

THE CRYPT

HALL without doors or windows, underground
Ancestral crypt of castle or keep; hewn stone
Of impregnable dream the strong walls of that state
Where unknown shadowy people come and go,
And I among them of my own free will,
Or by the will wherein my freedom's range
Brought to that place for reasons not my own.

So by the degrees of an approach
Whose slow steps crossed a distance not of space
But of a kind more arduous to traverse
I came to what seemed a bed or tomb of stone
Where a knight lay, or his effigy; not dead.
'King Amfortas,' told me some learned voice
Translating being's mystery into a name
That once could call to mind that nameless king deposed
Whom I in grave regions of the mind
Found where he lies lifelong on his bier.
I would have given help, had I known cause or cure
Of the deep ill that laid him on my bed of dream;
Must play what part I did not know, being there.

Then an old woman bowed with griefs and wrongs
Loudly in sorrowful histrionic voice complained and blamed;
I heard her unmoved; when she had said her say
Replied, 'All that you tell is true, but does not signify:
What of his guilt? All human guilt is nothing.'
For it seemed the causes of those ills lay deeper,
Or what she called wrongs were not wrongs at all.
I held my own with the people of dreams, and stood my
        human ground
Between unknowable cause and unknown outcome
Against that phantom of old wrongs forgotten.

Then it was I in my right hand beheld the sword
Whose diamond blade my weak wrist raised
Had passed through insubstantial dungeon walls,

Light of living light in my dark cave of sleep,
Gift shaped to my receiving, blinding to my blindness.
And on his bed of death the wounded knight
Stirred as with the first wave of an inflowing tide.
Slowly I sheathed that blade in an old scabbard.

HIEROS GAMOS

I DID not think to see them once again,
For what could bring into an old woman's dream
Canova's immarcescible marble lovers?
But, glimpsed and gone,
I knew what each in other adores in that enamoured
        smiling gaze.
They need no mirror of art whose bodies invest immortal joy,
Love for ever beholding beauty in imagination's sight.

It is said that some born blind
Can with sensitive finger-tips perceive the light,
All senses grown one sense, as angels, full of eyes;
Their hands do not possess nor mouths consume
Whose knowledge is the beloved being, and whose being, bliss;
Cupid and Psyche in their trance. Oblivion veiled too soon
From my ignorant animal sleep that nuptial mystery.

A DREAM OF ROSES

So many roses in the garden
Of last night's dream, and all were golden –
Ophelia's flowers of love forsaken,
Yellow rose of luckless loving
Or the golden flower of wisdom?

[173]

There, in a night of late November
Fantasy had grown so many
In a garden I had planted
(So the dream told me) long before.
Yet I searched among the gold
For even one of true rose colour,
And found none; dream cannot lie,
None I found of love's true flower.

THE RIVER

1

In my first sleep
I came to the river
And looked down
Through the clear water –
Only in dream
Water so pure,
Laced and undulant
Lines of flow
On its rocky bed
Water of life
Streaming for ever.

A house was there
Beside the river
And I, arrived,
An expected guest
About to explore
Old gardens and libraries –
But the car was waiting
To drive me away.

One last look
Into that bright stream –
Trout there were

And clear on the bottom
Monster form
Of the great crayfish
That crawls to the moon.
On its rocky bed
Living water
In whorls and ripples
Flowing unbounded.

There was the car
To drive me away.
We crossed the river
Of living water –
I might not stay,
But must return
By the road too short
To the waiting day.

2

IN my second dream
Pure I was and free
By the rapid stream,
My crystal house the sky,
The pure crystalline sky.

Into the stream I flung
A bottle of clear glass
That twirled and tossed and spun
In the water's race
Flashing the morning sun.

Down that swift river
I saw it borne away,
My empty crystal form,
Exultant saw it caught
Into the current's spin,
The flashing water's run.

TOLD IN A DREAM

'You have a hundred months to live,' I was told in a dream,
The speaker unknown, but the words plain:
Waking into this world, my death nearer than I had known.

What to the immortal signifies number or months or years?
Up and down the light is woven, a golden skein,
But how hold the living clue that runs time out of mind?

I, standing before the superhuman within, above me,
Glimpsed and gone, 'It will be enough,' replied,
Pledging my human time to enact a timeless will.

Little is enough, where of each part there is so great a whole;
Myself, or any self, must answer so,
What, of the poem I write, the life that lives me, can I know?

On a Deserted Shore

(1973)

Anima est ubi amat, non ubi animat.

The faint stars said,
'Our distances of night,
These wastes of space,
Sight can in an instant cross,

But who has passed
On soul's dark flight
Journeys beyond
The flash of our light.'

I said, 'Whence he is travelling
Let no heart's grief of mine
Draw back a thought
To these dim skies,

Nor human tears
Drench those wings that pass,
Freed from earth's weight
And the wheel of stars.'

WHERE my treasure is
        A grave:
My heart also
Empty.
            Sorrow
Is its own place, a glass
Of memories and dreams; a pool
Of tears. Narcissus pale
Sees his own drowning face.

2

From the hollow sphere of space
Echo
Of a lonely voice
That cries, my love, my love:
I do not know
Whether I spoke or heard
The word
That fills all silence.

3

I hid my heart
Within a certain stone
In a far mountain burn,
World-egg in its blue shell,
Invulnerable until
That pebble crushed,
Power and life were gone:
Not where we live but where we love, the soul.

4

What substance had Eurydice,
Or shade?
Unseen he knew that she was near
Whom when with bodily arms he held
Was waterfall, was fleeting flame, was empty air:
Yet in that country far
He only cast a shadow, bright was she.

5

I cannot weep
Who, when I turn to you in thought
Behold a mystery so deep,
A world upheld upon a breath
That comes in life and goes in death
Troubling dark leaves upon a starry bough.
Who dreams our lives I do not know,
Nor in what land it is we meet.

6

Memory: beyond recall
The linnet's song,
The clover-scented air;
Yet we were there,
My love and I together in one house.
Home is the sum of all
The days that sheltered us;
The place of no return.

7

Should some angel, turning the leaves
Of the closed book of lives
Open again those days solitary and sweet and wild,
Would not some essence pass, some chord
Tremble into the harmony of the spheres,
Lingering overtone of the remembered music that was ours?

8

The great whispering-gallery
Sends back strange echoes.
The desolate sends out a cry,
And there comes an answering voice
That utters the heart's mystery:
Does any heart reply?
Do we hear
The sea in the sound of a shell held to the inward ear?

9

How deep the recollection of the dead
In whose great memory we recall
The fabled story;
We taste the bitter fruit, we fail, we fall,
While earth's myriad buried hearts
Murmur forever in our ears
Music of undying joy.

·

10

Night. Moon. Black leaves.
I open the French window wide:
Between us other barriers,
Invisible, infinite.
On my threshold
When my window is open upon the night,
Moths, black leaves, moonlight.

11

Many and one: in the great memory
We know as we are known,
And you and I
Near as being to itself. Why then do we,
Waking to an ignorant day
Hear only in sleep
Sweet island voices that make us weep?

12

We who from day to day depart
From the country of the heart
In death return
To the fields our feet have travelled, our tears sown:
Sleeper beneath the rowan tree,
You have become your dream,
Sky, shore, and silver sea.

13

We do not hear the harmony
That sounds about us everywhere;
Sense bleeds on iron and thorns
Of rock and fire
Until death breaks the elemental forms
To free the music of the spheres
That builds all worlds continually.

14

They pass into that music:
I too in sleep have heard
The harmony sublime
And known myself among the blessed dead.
We cannot walk the waves they tread,
For the earth of heaven is sound,
To sense this stony ground:
They hear as music what we feel as pain.

15

Under the budding boughs
Beyond a grave he stood:
She took him for the gardener who mows
The springing grass,
But then saw, he it was
Who grows the living from the dead.

16

I like a traveller have passed
Through days and years
Stranger and guest of many lives,
And came at last
To my love's place and time,
Dreamed I had come home,
But waking stood by a grave-side.

17

A grave:
Loves' bitter fruit
And buried seed,
Sanctuary inviolate
Of unborn life.

18

No title mine to mourn –
From my own memories exiled
Since you on later friends bestowed
Those regions of your dreams and mine
Interwoven in one world.
That finespun texture rent,
Invisible sanctuary torn down,
Where but in sorrow shall I hide?

19

If many, how lonely,
Even in requited love how far
Each heart from other;
But if one the whole, and we
Leaves on that great tree,
And weary time a flow in starry veins,
Nourished from hidden roots, and blossoming boughs
Where birds of heaven rest,
Then no love lost.

20

Rigid, naked, pale —
Body's friend and guest,
Where now your abiding-place,
Gentle wandering soul?

21

Cold comfort for the heart:
I read the books, I acquiesce,
Plotinus on the soul's descent,
Iamblichus on the Mysteries,
The Indian, German, and the Greek:
Knowledge a cold mirror where forms pass
That only seem to move and speak.

22

Mist-dwellers:
Love in part remembers,
But who we are,
And where before our eyes had met –
In soul's far wanderings
What is that glory we forget?

23

In heart's truth I declare
What most I fear
To find beyond death's veil:
Not legendary hells of ice and fire
But a face too merciful
For my own devil-peopled soul to bear.

24

So far –
Out of the night
We travelled, you and I,
To meet on this small star.
Our chosen fate,
Our meed and sole desire
All we have lost.

25

Not to be unbarred:
I beat upon the gate,
And every way the dark:
Bonds I cannot break,
Hooded hawk
Of my spirit.

26

People of dreams:
As in a glass we meet,
Darkly: I the ghost whose haunt
Is your bright fields.

27

When empty seas and winds and distances
Divided us
I still could turn my face
And say, that way he lies.
I have no compass now
To tell me where beyond the multitude of stars
Lost Paradise.

28

Enough the day – had I, a child
Under the wide sky
Happy when petals opened or bird sang
Foreknown my human part,
That I must hurt and harm
And bring to naught,
Never had I known joy.

29

Unseen fingers cool as hyacinth-roots
Dislimn the clay
Of soul's long-loved discarded mortal face:
She of graves,
Whose secret alchemy
Brings all our ends to her immaculate source.

30

How many faces have your worn,
Life after life,
By human passion
Obscured and torn? None
So dear, my love,
As I knew by your name.

31

Water of life
That wells from some deep vein
Beneath the graves,
Beneath the roots of sorrow –
Music its flow:
Whence comes whither goes
Joy, whose source none knows?

32

Not mine the joy
That pours its melody
Over my rocky bed: how long its flow
Before the stone I am turned to
Is worn away?

33

Mountain and tree and bird,
And that pure stream –
How beautifully the world
Mirrored back to us
An ancient dream:
The dreamer gone,
Nature an empty glass.

34
Away, away,
Unhealing time,
Since you can bring no day
When my love and I,
Though I should wait life-long
On lonely shores,
Can meet again.

35
Banished from that bright dream
Of the heart's truth,
Betrayed by all that we have done and been,
Sorrow still keeps faith.

36
Truth comes full circle
As departing light
From infinite space
Returns to the heart
Still what it was,
Embracing all.

37
Truth is echo's voice
In whose resonance
Question answers question,
Hate to hate replies,
Confusion to confusion,
Cry to cry cries.

38

Despair – we approach but never reach
That quiet place.
The suicidal leap
Invokes a mercy earth denies:
It is hope
That wakes to anguish
And will not let us sleep.

39

Hope and despair – the scope
Of what we are,
Height and deep
Each mirroring other:
Infinite desire
The far fall we fear,
Heaven, hell, the angel's ladder,
The dead man's drop.

40

Blessed who mourn,
For love is comforted
In every station of the heart:
It is enough
That on the stone of earth
The print of feet.

41

How many buried hearts
Instruct me when I speak
Of that long pilgrimage
The soul must walk
On bleeding feet
Who has in folly lost
One whom in bitter after-wisdom she must seek.

42

So many scattered leaves
The Sibyl shakes
From the living tree.
Gather who will her oracles,
Believe who may –
All truths are lies
Save love to love in love replies.

43

Lost Paradise
With all its trees adrift
In the great flood of night,
And I live yet
Not knowing where in emptiness
Landfall lies.

44

A night in a bad inn –
But I would say
Guest in love's house;
And blessed and thrice blest
Who walk on earth's sweet grass,
Bathe in time's stream,
And under green boughs rest –
Too short a stay.

45

For the beat of a heart
A world, a dream endures,
Yet on this earth we met,
And every stone is dear
That wounds love's pilgrim feet
Walking the way of time's
Six thousand years.

46

Longing of lips and thighs –
A grave apart,
For arms' embrace too wide,
Or fingers' touch.
The language of the flesh
Too faintly cries:
And yet no lover lies
As the dead so close at heart.

47

Strange bird across my evening sky –
Who, passing soul, your guide
On that far flight
Beyond earth's dwindling star?
With certainty of strong desire
You wing your traceless way
Into harbourless night.

48

They shall be comforted, he said,
Who sent the comforter
To those who mourned him, dead:
What comfort could he send,
He being crucified,
Unless himself, who died?

49

The last sorrow silent –
Forgetfulness
That feels no loss,
No hope discerns,
Saddest impoverishment
When deepest memories fade
And all love's tears are dust.

50

Dear angel of my birth,
All my life's loss,
Gold of fallen flowers,
Shells after ebbing wave
Gathered on lonely shores
With secret toil of love,
Deathless in memory save
The treasures of my grave.

51

Time was
When each to other was a glass,
And I in you and you in me beheld
Lost Paradise,
With every tree and bird so clear
Regained it seemed:
We did not guess how far
From the heart's mirror the reflected star.

52

Illusion all –
Yet where for us the real
Unless what seems?
These cloud-capped towers
More durable than brass
Our dreams.

53

Say I must recognize
I but imagined love
Where no love was,
Say all is a dream
In whose brief span
Childhood, womanhood, the grave
Where my love lies:
That dream is all I am.

54

Cast not before swine –
The rational animal
Oysters' soft aphrodisiac flesh prefers:
Who values then a pearl
At so great price
As to sell all
To purchase one?

55

Mussel-pearls
From Sandaig shore
Held in a shell
As God worlds
In the palm of his hand:
These our treasure,
Sea-life's toil,
Seed more rare
Than barren sand.

56
What infinitely precious thing
Did we seek along the shore?
What signature,
Promise in pearly shell, wisdom in stone?
What dead king's golden crown, tide-worn,
What lost imperishable star?

57
Silence of the dead;
The untold:
What would you have me say?
Dear love, when we on earth kept house together
Were you then this mystery?

58
If fancy cannot cheat
The fevered flesh, the aching heart,
Can sense the dream
With lineaments of dust?
From Paradise
The bird's undying voice
Sings on.

59
She who in cold elemental arms upbore
Her prince to shore
Yet did not win his heart
Bought dear these mortal feet;
Must pay love's price: how else
Shall an immortal walk in sorrow's ways?

60

I would not change my grief
For any joy:
Sorrow the secret bond
The signature of blood
That seals to you my life
Indissolubly.

61

From long ago returned,
As my lost self you seemed:
Of lover's play what need
For children gazing in a stream
Bright head by golden head?

62

Ah, burning boy,
In winter's night
To me you came,
You seemed to supplicate, but I,
Reaching with mortal arms to your cold fire,
Could not come near
Your place of pain.

63

I see you in mind's eye,
A man of light:
How faint and far away
Your face that blesses me.

64

Image of an image, shade of shade,
In memory or dream,
Time future or time past,
In this or any world or state of being,
Shall we who parted
Meet at last?

65

Sea-change:
The grain of pain
Love layer on layer enspheres;
Sorrow its gradual pearl
Perfects with life-long toil
Beneath the tides.

66

Dark stream.
I did not know
When to your brink I came
How full your flow
Of the world's sorrow:
I dip my cup and drink.

67

A prison, a paradise –
Tell me, dear friend,
Beyond those gates never to be unbarred, where pass
A people of dreams,
This world, which now it seems?

68

By dreams uncomforted
I wake to this blank day:
Free-will, fixed fate,
Foreknowledge, providence,
And life astray,
All possibility
Narrowed to this weary bed.

69

Already it has changed –
Dear love, you would not know the place.
I look for you in memory's house,
But there too rooms grow vague.

70

Yellow iris by the shore,
Burnish of wing and golden eye,
Green-gold birch and, gold on water,
Sun's bright rings hand could not hold,
You will not see this spring, nor I,
Nor in the bay the rocking eider,
All wasted and all spent, that gold.

71

Heart's memories –
Rooms I cannot enter more,
Green ways by the water:
Joy once ours
Sings in the wind that stirs the grass.

72
Always just beyond –
The next wave will lift its deep-sea treasure to the strand,
The next flower open golden centre, stone be star.
And yet the near how far
From whose green sanctuary
The ousel flings its wild wind-drifted song.
From body's blindfold free,
Have you, lost seeker, found?

73
We were of a kind, nearer
You were than brother,
Whose hand clasped mine,
Now dust; your land
Beyond the heart's dark night.

74
Of a kind, living and dead;
For as you are, or are not, all must be;
And if the dead be not,
How came you here, my child,
With wisdom in your heart, and crowned with joy?

75
Little of what you were, less of myself I knew,
Loved with my blind heart I knew not who,
Nor from what root love's recognition grew,
Who in my ignorance worshipped and wounded you.

76
What the hand holds –
So little of time's flow
The all we know;
But from their hearts who pass,
The lifelong moment breaks
Into death's boundless now:
Shelterless their state, and ours.

77
Arid bilbergia's rigid leaves
Describe each its parabola. Slow the flow
Water takes from air, air from swirling space,
Comes to its term, to standstill dies.
As above, so below,
Traced by figures of the dancing stars.

78
Shadow of hills on the still loch, mysterious
Inviolate green land, whose sun is cool as water,
Whose stones bruise not,
Seems soul's native place, this weary road
The dark country in a glass.

79
Your garment cast away,
This body's clay
The grave that shrouds from sight
The man of light,
Bright, but how far you are.

80

Flash again, golden wing,
Across my sterile plot,
Seeking in vain
Similitude of glade and dell.
Where human passions dwell
Few flowers spring,
Too far from that remembered hill.

81

If I could wake
From bitter life as from a dream,
In innocence new-born
To see the first day break,
The promise of the eternal dawn
Would bear your name.

82

Original sin:
I stand condemned, being born,
To cast the human shadow;
We darken each our sun,
Who have not done, but are, that wrong.

83

Two wanderers in a single dream
By paths of gold on silver seas
We to lost Paradise came home,
Together stood beneath those blossoming trees,
But went our ways
Uncomforted, and each alone.

84

Memories: shrivelled leaves
To keep or throw away.
Love cannot piece by piece
Remake the felled tree.

85

From your grave-side
All ways lead away,
And time is long, my love,
And memories fade,
Old hearts grow cold:
Must I too break faith
With joy?

86

Sad and strange
Are the dreams of the old,
Joyless and cold
Those chambers underground.
Ghost among ghosts I range
Catacombs of the mind
And neither find nor seek,
Nor laugh nor weep.

87

Hard is the way
To your unvisited house,
Barred the gates. Some say
To love is given the key
Of memory, the grave, Paradise.

88

This empty world too small,
Heart's void too great,
Everywhere visible the wall,
Nowhere the gate.

89

'Till death us part,' the young promise:
Too short a wedding-day.
Life parted us; too long a loneliness
For those who wait
Outside love's sanctuary.

90

What mist falls between
Two who have seen
One in other the eternal face?
What violation
Shatters the bright mirror
Lover holds to lover,
Or blindness darks the glass?

91

Does that Judgment seem less dread,
The Judge more merciful,
Each being to ourselves
Accuser and accused,
And heaven and hell?

92

All seems the same;
But this familiar room
Stands in the years we shared,
Where I, a ghost
Out of this unreal future, haunt
The long-past present that was home.

93

Heart's truth: from shelving depths
Shaped by the weight of sorrow where it broods,
Sightless surfaces,
Tormented by the sun,
Love's monster weeping form.

94

Heart's truth: a moment out of time,
Pollen-grain adrift,
How small and fine,
Golden upon the spirit's breath
Into that quiet chamber sown.

95

The resurrection of the dead:
Into what strange land
Are you, beside whose empty grave I stand
New-born, my child?

96
Heart turns into its night
Scanning the darkest quarter for the dawn
Of a sun that set:
Else there is none.

97
If I could turn
Upon my finger the bright ring of time,
The now of then
I would bring back again.

98
Since smoke rose from your pyre
All clouds are dear; but how
Among those vague bright forms,
Yours shall I know?

99
'In spirit accompany me.'
– Your parting words by heart I know.
On what far journey then do we
Into the dark together go?

100
Into your boundless state
All night afloat
On lift and fall of the great sea
Rocks in the bay my anchored boat.

101

As myself: so once
When hand in hand.
I here, you in no place
That such as I can find,
Living and dead,
Still of a kind.

102

Beyond the empty door
Spaces, distances, stars
Innumerable, beautiful and far;
Mysterious night over us.
The darkness too His house, and ours.

103

Out of the arms of night
None can fall,
Refuge of sinners
Whose merciful stars towards us
Beam from their height
Indifference
Absolving all.

104

Ended my earthly day,
And with averted face
I from your graveside turn away
Into a veiled, a secret place.

105
Over your mountain isle
Streaming cloud
Shrouds the sunset:
A shawl drawn close
Over a mourner's head.

106
Great the domain of love:
Farther than eye can see
From my small house of life
Realms of your new state encompass me.

107
Sun gives no light
And days like shadows pass.
Shut by the lids of sense, my blinded gaze
Cannot discern your spirit bright.

108
Cadence of an old song from Eriskay
Tells the heart's story:
From dissonance of the world I turn away
Not to evade but to descry
Lineaments of humanity.

109

Grief's metamorphoses:
Anguish, small pregnant seed,
Becomes a worm that gnaws through years,
At last quiescent lies; not dead;
Till waking, what winged impulse takes the skies?

110

'Made to be broken,' a lover said
Who knew the heart
That breaks and breaks again,
And yet will not believe
That love is born to grief.

111

Not sorrow breaks the heart
But an imagined joy
So dear it cannot be
But we have elsewhere known
The lost estate we mourn.

112

Whole that has made me,
Whose stress and weight
Creates and will destroy,
Each part, I find,
Bears always all the world.

113

Downcast on the ground,
The form of spirit
We are but do not know
Save by a shadow
Distorted, earthbound.

114

You who cast no shadow, nowhere, everywhere,
All that you loved you are,
Sun's gold on the sea, waves far out from the shore,
Flowing for ever.

115

Blue serene wide sky
Where sight runs free, joy
Of unbounded light:
It is as if we meet.

116

Dream, shadow of hope and fear,
Secret foreshadower, guide
Of all souls, living and dead,
What the unwinding and inwinding thread
But heart's desire?

117

I am content to be
At last what first we were,
Grass of the one hill,
Water of the one pool,
Breath of the same air,
Sight of the single eye.

118

The Nine Nicks rose out of the past
Into this after day.
'You have been long away,'
They said, 'can you forget
We in his life had part,
Speak to you from his heart?'

119

We walked in the same dream:
Do you, awake,
Dissolving clouds recall of hills once home
That sheltered us in sleep
Whose desolate ways I tread alone?

120

At the last leap I shrink
From fall of black sea-cliff and moiling water, wake
To find in grey of dawn vague leaves and roses break
In foam of that far sea.
On lip of petal, margin of leaf, that brink.

121

Somewhere, it seems,
You who walk with me in sleep;
But in the sand of dreams
Your passing leaves no trace
To follow or find that place.

122

If I could follow you,
How find?
In number's starry flow
Of all night's multitude, what lot
Once cast us heart to heart?

123

Ah near at heart:
Far star's reflection in a well
Is still
Light.

124

At the end of fear
Out over that black skerry,
Regions of wind and moiling sea:
How long will mortal terror
Withhold, imprison me?

125

If hope could dare
All heart's desire
Bright hills how fair
Despair would build
In empty air.

126

Whisperer in the wind –
From what dream do you look upon this shore
Grown strange and fair and far?
Rain walks with heavier tread,
In rustle of grass you are,
Then not.

127

Near and far, summit and sky,
Soaring wing, circling joy,
Thrilling bird-voice over the bay,
You their bright presence,
Dazzle of blue waves' dance,
Gold of the silver sea.

128

Opening a vanished door
I move on insubstantial feet
About your window, desk and chair,
Reviving each familiar object there.
Do memories of the living build
Memory-houses of the dead,
A place at heart where we may meet?

129

That we die who live
My heart knew by your grave.
Does he live who died?
'He is not here,' the angel on the stone replied.

130

Faith, shadow of desire
Some hold; but I
Who angelic hearsay fear
To live by,
Yet know that only the listening ear
The gazing eye
Can the far descry.

Suddenly the trees looked strangely beautiful:
'It has taken the form of trees,' I said,
'And I of a woman standing by a burn.'
So near I stood to your new state
I saw for a moment as you might
These sheltering boughs of spirit in its flight.
Shall you and I, in all the journeyings of soul,
Remember the rowan tree, the waterfall?

The Oval Portrait

(1977)

MUSIC

Ah, beautiful intangible
Country we can set no foot upon,
Nor kiss that earth, nor lay body down on
To weep, or sleep, or lie in grave,
No, nor by footfall come home,
Travelling out of time on these Mozartian waves,
Whose heavy hearts beat base
To so high heavenly a treble and multiple concord.

AUTUMN

Leaf-fall,
And the longed-for missed again
Between the coming and the gone;
Yet in tree's thinning leaves the crown
In this faded year-worn scrawl,
Blade's blot, bare stroke of petiole
Wind-tattered on a ragged sky
Stands ciphered still.

DREAM

How did I come, last night,
To that great mansion of the dead,
Night-house whose empty rooms were dense with fear?
Why did I dread their presences, who had been dear,
My heart throb with terror
Lest I see faces not human
That once shone on me with familiar love?

Secret companion
Whose face I have never seen,
Absent these many years,
Have you been sad, as I, that we no longer
As once, wander bright fields together?
Do daimons mourn to see
Earthly charges stray away
Into blind mists and shadowy cities,
Lost on strange roads of time, detours, blind turnings?
Have you, invisible one,
Learned from my life-long story the sad wisdom
Of earth, and stilled the song
That once I heard at heart?
Or will you, on a dream's frontier,
Return and speak to me some morning,
And let us comfort one another?
Tell me again of spirit's undying joy,
And I will tell how we who walk the world
In merciful forgetfulness traverse
Moment by moment, little by little, this great plane of sorrow.

NOVEMBER DREAM

I wake to sycamore's yellowing leaves against the grey
Of cloud and London brick,
Day's solid walls and faintly luminous sky;
And still I almost see, in mind's eye,
Last night's woodland way
I followed under boughs of gold
Bathed in another light than these
That stand outside my window's narrow space.

No separation set me there, as here, apart
From dream's afresh-created sky and trees.
In that remembered country I was there indeed
While here, in body locked away,
Touch solid wood, wet leaves, earth-coloured flowers
And all is other that I feel and see;
Yet this world we call real, that has no place.

WHAT IS IT TO BE OLD . . .

WHAT is it to be old
But to dwell in far places
Among young faces,
Young voices and laughter,
Young prowess and pride of feature
In the remembered gardens, the familiar houses
Of the dead.

ACACIA TREE

DAY by day the acacia tree
With gold of noon and evening sun
Through airy quivering leaves made play
In shadow underleaf, and gay

Mirrors tossing blades of light
Various before your failing sight.
Four pigeons plumed in rose and grey
Browsed spring buds of the tree's crown
And heavy white and fragrant flowers
To petal-fall in summer hung
Until mid-August's dulling leaves
Began to cast their yellow coin.

As time for you ran swift away
Moment by moment, day to night,
Nature's illuminated book,
No two moving hours the same,
Lay always open at one page
Where Tree in its long present stood,
September day by golden day.
Only before eyes new-born,
Eyes fading, does the mystery stay,
A presence neither come nor gone.

THE OVAL PORTRAIT:
Jessie Wilkie, 1880–1973

AT eighteen, you stood for this faded photograph,
Your young hand awkwardly holding the long skirt
Over that light foot no trammelling at your heels could stay,
The constricting blouse framing in the eighteen-nineties
The young girl whose round sweet face,
Soft shining curls piled above fine brows and wild-bird's eyes
Has such a proud air of freedom and happy heart.

You were in love, that day,
Only with the beautiful world, that lay,
You thought, in your life's untold story,
As you, fledged for womanhood, ready to soar,
Stood poised before the camera's dark glass
Untouched by the shadow sorrow casts before
On all such inviolate light-heartedness.

Those young eyes, unfaded by your ninety years
Still saw in each day earth's wonders new-begun,
Each yesterday a leaf sinking into a dark pool
Of a swift sky-reflecting burn.
All for you was always the first time, or the last,

Every parting for evermore, but free each happy return
Of memory's unforgiveness, memory's remorse.

Your spirit fast in time's jesses, still you turned
On death's camera obscura that proud look,
Expectant, though not unafraid; after his first stroke
'I was interested', you said; as the goshawk,
Its hood lifted then drawn down again
Over the golden eyes, is restless to go free
On unencumbered wings home to its wilderness.

CARD-TABLE

ALWAYS you were ready, revived by a good cup of tea,
To open the leaves of the folding table into a world
And from your rosewood box inlaid with ivory
Brought out the cards, the markers, or the board,
Switched off the flicker of the television screen
Where blacks and whites merge into indifferent grey
For an emblematic country where you, its queen,
Moved pawns and kings in errantry
Of ebony Spenserian knights and horses trapped in gold
Whose sovereigns held in check imperious heart and sword
And the invisible reaper delved his single spade
For lords of castle perilous and dark tower,
Your pitched court, your ever-embattled realm.

You liked to win; I too, though with less passion
Than you whose real world was all imagination
Untarnished by those ninety years that dimmed your sight and locked
    your fingers
While you and I wore out whole packs and sets of great ones
As tide of fortune ebbed and flowed, or skill prevailed
For you, by luck or extra-sensory perception favoured,
(Familiarly by your Scottish theologians named Old Nick).
But no sermons could restrain those wild ancestors of yours

[223]

From poetry, whisky, games of chance with cards or dams
Or their own brave blood-gilt persons ventured on the field
With no reprieve, honour and pride at stake
And hearts to mourn when knaves prevailed.
How well you would have played their reckless gamblers' game of life!
Now what a world of magic with that box is shut.

YOUR GIFT OF LIFE WAS IDLENESS...

YOUR gift of life was idleness,
As you would set day's task aside
To marvel at an opening bud,
Quivering leaf, or spider's veil
On dewy grass in morning spread.
These were your wandering thoughts, that strayed
Across the ever-changing mind
Of airy sky and travelling cloud,
The harebell and the heather hill,
World without end, where you could lose
Memory, identity and name
And all that you beheld, became,
Insect wing and net of stars
Or silver-glistering wind-borne seed
For ever drifting free from time.
What has unbounded life to do
With body's grave and body's womb,
Span of life and little room?

THE LEAF

'How beautifully it falls,' you said,
As a leaf turned and twirled
On invisible wind upheld,
How airily to ground
Prolongs its flight.

You for a leaf-fall forgot
Old age, loneliness,
Body's weary frame,
Crippled hands, failing sense,
Unkind world and its pain.

What did that small leaf sign
To you, troth its gold
Plight 'twixt you and what unseen
Messenger to the heart
From a fair, simple land?

HER ROOM

At first, not breathed on,
Not a leaf or a flower knew you were gone,
Then, one by one,

The little things put away,
The glass tray
Of medicines empty,

The poems still loved
Long after sight failed
With other closed books shelved,

And from your cabinet
Remembrances to one and another friend
Who will forget

How the little owl, the rose-bowl,
The Brig-o' Doone paperweight,
The Japanese tea-set

Lived on their shelf, just here,
So long, and there,
Binding memories together,

Binding your love,
Husband and daughter in an old photograph,
Your woven texture of life

A torn cobweb dusted down,
Swept from the silent room
That was home.

WITH A WAVE OF HER OLD HAND ...

WITH a wave of her old hand
She put her past away,
Ninety years astray
In time's fading land,

With that dismissive gesture
Threw off pretence,
Rose to her proud stature,
Had done with world's ways,

Had done with words,
Closed her last written book
To ponder deeper themes
In unrecorded dreams.

STORM-STAYED

HOLY, holy, holy is the light of day
The grey cloud, the storm wind, the cold sea,
Holy, holy the snow on the mountain,
Holy the stone, the dry heather, the stunted tree,
Holy the heron and the hoodie, holy
The leaf and the rain,
The cold wind and the cold wave, cold light of day
And the turning of earth from night into morning,
Holy this place where I am,
The last house, it may be,
Before the wind, the shelterless sky, the unbounded sea.

FOR THE VISITOR'S BOOK

Canna House, 1975
For John and Margaret

THE cards that brighten the New Year,
A Christmas-tree grown in the wood,
The crimson curtains drawn, the owl
Whose porcelain holds a lamp to read
The music on the Steinway grand
Piano with its slipping scores
Of Couperin, Chopin and Ravel –
John and Margaret Campbell made
This room to house the things they treasure,
Records of Scotland's speech and song,
Lore of butterfly and bird,
And velvet cats step soft among
Learned journals on the floor.

More formal state across the hall,
The silver of the house displayed,
And ivory ladies, Chinese birds

[227]

Surveyed by Romney's General
Sir Archibald, whose following eyes
Seem with cool justice to appraise
Guests of the house who come and go.
His scarlet, silver order, sword,
Give him the advantage as he stands
Relaxed, imperial Madras
His pictured background, ours a world
That now breeds few he would approve,
That kindly but commanding man
Who played the part his rank assigned
And governed by a law deemed just
As Indian Arjuna before,
Taught by his god to act, though slain
And slayer were of equal worth.
The rule of duty had not changed
With other empire, other race,
Though oftener in our day ignored
By innovators, who to make
A new world would destroy old ways.

In Scotland it is Hogmanay
Most warms the feelings of the heart,
Religion older than the old,
The cycle of perpetual things
In years that pass and years to come.
Here children sing from memory
Ancestral island tunes that praise
Those best of loves that never change
Though new men bear their fathers' names,
Boatmen and herdsmen of these shores.
We feast on venison from a neighbouring hill
Under that Campbell general's eye,
The drone of pipes across the bay,
The pibroch, 'Cattle of Kintail'
Played by the piper of the isle.

MAIRE MACRAE'S SONG

THE singer is old and has forgotten
Her girlhood's grief for the young soldier
Who sailed away across the ocean,
Love's brief joy and lonely sorrow:
The song is older than the singer.

The song is older than the singer
Shaped by the love and the long waiting
Of women dead and long forgotten
Who sang before remembered time
To teach the unbroken heart its sorrow.

The girl who waits for her young soldier
Learns from the cadence of a song
How deep her love, how long the waiting.
Sorrow is older than the heart,
Already old when love is young:
The song is older than the sorrow.

DESERTED VILLAGE ON MINGULAY

From a photograph by Margaret Fay Shaw Campbell

NOT far had men's hands to raise from the stony ground
Blocks the ice and rain had hewn.
The dry-stone walls of the houses of Mingulay still stand
Long after the sheltering roof is gone.
Not far had the heather thatch to blow back to the moor.

Children were born here, women sang
Their songs in an ancient intricate mode
As they spun the wool of sheep on the hill
By a bog turf fire hot on the swept hearth-stone.
Earth's breast that nourished and warmed was near
As cow-byre and lazy-bed
Made fertile with sea-wrack carried up from the shore

[229]

In creels of withies cut in a little glen,
Near as shelter of hill-side, fragrance of clover-scented air.

Not far had the dead to go on their way of return,
Not far the circle of the old burial-ground
Whose low wall sets its bound to encroaching wild
That never has put on pride of human form,
Worn face of maiden or fisherman, mother or son.
Never far the washer of shrouds, the hag with grey hair;
Yet those who here lived close to the mother of all
Found, it may be, in her averted face, little enough to fear.

BINAH

LIFELONG the way –
I never thought to reach her throne
In darkness hidden, starless night
Her never-lifted veil;
Too far from what I am
That source, sacred, secret from day;   *
But, suddenly weeping, remembered
Myself in her embrace,
In her embrace who was my own
Mother, my own mother, in whose womb
Human I became.
Not far, I found, but near and simple as life,
Loved in the beginning, beyond praise
Your mothering of me in flesh and blood.
Deep her night, but never strange
Who bore me out of the kind animal dark
Where safe I lay, heart to heartbeat, as myself
Your stream of life carrying me to the world.
Remote your being as the milky way,
Yet fragrance not of temple incense nor symbolic rose
Comforted me, but your own,
Whose soft breasts, nipples of earth, sustained me,

Mortal, in your everlasting arms.
Known to the unborn, to live is to forget
You, our all,
Whose unseen sorrowing face is a farewell,
Forgotten forgiver of forgetfulness.
Lifelong we seek that longed-for unremembered place.

NOT THAT I HAVE FORGOTTEN...

Not that I have forgotten,
Not that those poignant days
From the long present of the world are gone,
But that I no more choose to open
My book of life to scan
The record of lost years until the last is written.
Then, being freed from time, as the dead are,
I will be again
Where every tide-wet shell, each intricate ripple of the
        running burn,
Scent of birch in the first thaw of spring, remain;
To the very place and hour
Someday, with you, return.

I WENT OUT IN THE NAKED NIGHT...

I went out in the naked night
And stood where you had often stood,
And called you where the winter moon
Over Canna harbour rode
Clear of the sheltering wind-bent trees
Above the quivering Pleiades
Where once at anchor rocked your boat.

The mountain isles changeless and still
As memory's insubstantial strand:
May not the living and the dead
Meet where dreaming spirit turns
To the sea-wracked remembered shore,
Revisiting this welcoming door,
Crushed shells beneath your grounding keel?

The moonlit waters of the bay
Move under the December stars
Between the shores of earth and dream.
In the unending Now of night,
In being's one unbroken theme
Your presence and my present meet:
I hold my transient breath to hear
The crunch of shells beneath your feet.

EIDER AFLOAT IN THE BAY . . .

EIDER afloat in the bay,
Cloud-capped isles far out,
This thyme-sweet turf I tread,
Real under my feet,

These were your world,
Your loved and known;
Can you recall to mind
Wrack-strewn shore and tide-wet stone?

I seek you in wave-wrought shell,
In wild bird's eye:
What country have the dead
But memory?

We who travel time
Call past and gone
Remembered days that those who dream
Call home.

CROSSING THE SOUND . . .

CROSSING the sound I summoned you in thought
To look out of my eyes at sea and sky,
Soft clouds sheltering those hills that once you knew
And sea-paths where you sailed,
The white birds following your boat from isle to isle.
Would it have seemed to you still beautiful, this world?
Or from that other state
Do you discern a darkness in our light,
The cloud of blood that veils our skies,
And in the labouring wings of hungry gulls
The weight of death? If it be so,
Dear love, I would not call you back
To bear again the heaviness of earth
Upon the impulse of your joy,
Locked in a living skull your thought,
Your vision shut with human eyes.

ALL THAT IS . . .

ALL that is:
The unbroken surface of the sea
Bears ships and isles,
Shell-duck and eider in the bay;
Wings soar, wild voices cry.

Shining waves
Cast up fresh shells
On the sweet turf that covers the fine sand
Of innumerable gleaming lives.
Light fills all space
And all life joy,
All shores the sea: no place
For what has ceased to be.

BLUE BUTTERFLIES' EYED WINGS . . .

BLUE butterflies' eyed wings,
Eyed buzzard high in blue sky,
Mountain isles blue veiled
In fleeting shade of fleeting cloud,
Of these I am the I.

PETAL OF WHITE ROSE . . .

PETAL of white rose
And rosy shell
Cast up by the tide:
Who can tell
This burnet sweetness
From memory,
From the deep sea
Record of a life
Shaped by the restless wave.

ON BASALT ORGAN-PIPES . . .

ON basalt organ-pipes
The wind tunes harmonies.
Sweet humming voices rise and fall
In murmur of the rocks and the wind's choir.
I overheard them singing
The song few hear
But the buzzard on the crag, the rabbit on the hill.

TURNER'S SEAS

We call them beautiful
Turner's appalling seas, shipwreck and deluge
Where man's contraptions, mast and hull,
Lurch, capsize, shatter to driftwood in the whelming surge and swell,
Men and women like spindrift hurled in spray
And no survivors in those sliding glassy graves.
Doomed seafarers on unfathomed waters,
We yet call beautiful those gleaming gulphs that break in foam,
Beautiful the storm-foreboding skies, the lurid west,
Beautiful the white radiance that dissolves all.
What recognition from what deep source cries
Glory to the universal light that walks the ever-running waves,
What memory deeper than fear, what recollection of untrammelled joy
Our scattered falling drops retain of gleaming ocean's unending play?

THE POET ANSWERS THE ACCUSER

No matter what I am,
For if I tell of winter lightning, stars and hail,
Of white waves, pale Hebridean sun,
It is not I who see, who hear, who tell, but all
Those cloud-born drops the scattering wind has blown
To be regathered in the stream of ocean,
The many in the one;
For these I am,
Water, wind and stone I am,
Grey birds that ride the storm and the cold waves I am,
And what can my words say,
Who am a drop in ocean's spray,
A bubble of white foam,
Who am a breath of wandering air,
But what the elements in me cry
That in my making take their joy,

In my unmaking go their way?
I am, but do not know, my song,
Nor to what scale my sense is tuned
Whose music trembles through me and flows on.
A note struck by the stars I am,
A memory-trace of sun and moon and moving waters,
A voice of the unnumbered dead, fleeting as they –
What matter who I am?

CLOUD

Never alone
While over unending sky
Clouds move for ever.
Calling them beautiful
Humanity is in love with creatures of mist.
Borne on the wind they rest,
Tenuous, without surface,
Passive stream from shape to shape,
Being with being melting breast with cloudy breast.
Ah could we like these
In freedom move in peace on the commotion of the air,
Never to return to what we are.
Made, unmade, remade, at rest in change,
From visible to invisible they pass
Or gather over the desolate hills
Veils of forgetfulness
Or with reflected splendour evening grey
Charged with fiery gold and burning rose,
Their watery shapes shrines of the sun's glory.

WINTER PARADISE

Now I am old and free from time
How spacious life,
Unbeginning unending sky where the wind blows
The ever-moving clouds and clouds of starlings on the wing,
Chaffinch and apple-leaf across my garden lawn,
Winter paradise
With its own birds and daisies
And all the near and far that eye can see,
Each blade of grass signed with the mystery
Across whose face unchanging everchanging pass
Summer and winter, day and night.
Great countenance of the unknown known
You have looked upon me all my days,
More loved than lover's face,
More merciful than the heart, more wise
Than spoken word, unspoken theme
Simple as earth in whom we live and move.

HARVEST OF LEARNING ...

Harvest of learning I have reaped,
Fruits of many a life-time stored,
The false discarded, proven kept,
Knowledge that is its own reward –
　　No written page more true
　　Than blade of grass and drop of dew.

Striven my partial self to bind
Within tradition great and whole,
Christendom's two thousand years,
Wisdom's universal mind –
　　No doctrine heart can heal
　　As cloudless sky and lonely hill.

Now I am old my books I close
And forget religion's ties,
Untrammelled the departing soul
Puts out of mind both false and true,
    Distant hills and spacious skies,
    Grass-blade and morning dew.

THE VERY LEAVES OF THE ACACIA TREE...

THE very leaves of the acacia tree are London;
London tap-water fills out the fuchsia buds in the back garden,
Blackbirds pull London worms out of the sour soil,
The woodlice, centipedes, eat London, the wasps even.
London air through stomata of myriad leaves
And million lungs of London breathes.
Chlorophyll and haemoglobin do what life can
To purify, to return this great explosion
To sanity of leaf and wing.
Gradual and gentle the growth of London Pride,
And sparrows are free of all the time in the world:
Less than a window-pane between.

AFTERNOON SUNLIGHT PLAYS...

AFTERNOON sunlight plays
Through trailing leaves I cannot see,
Stirred by a little wind that mixes light and leaf
To filter their quiet pattern on my floor.
Not real, Plato said, the shadowy dancers,
Imponderable,
Somewhere beyond, the light; but I am old,
Content with these shadows of shadows that visit me,
Present unsummoned, gone without stir.

So angels, it may be.

BRIGHT CLOUD . . .

BRIGHT cloud,
Bringer of rain to far fields,
To me, who will not drink that waterfall nor feel
Wet mist on my face,
White gold and rose
Vision of light,
Meaning and beauty immeasurable.
That meaning is not rain, nor that beauty mist.

FROM

The Oracle in the Heart

(1980)

I WHO AM . . .

I WHO am what the dead have made,
The violent story they recall
Must understand, must suffer all
Their distant clamorous voices cry.

There's no escaping them – I run
But still they follow with my feet,
Stubborn they bend me to their toil.
Temper to their need my will.

My mother's mother blacked her grate;
Fallen, my father's sister died:
What old obsession drives me still
To appease desire ungratified?

A drunkard schoolmaster who cast
His fishing-line with feathered fly,
Whose solace was the rippling salmon-river –
I watch a leaf turn on an eddy with his eye.

What grief untold framed me to endure
The age-old longing I obey?
What hope of theirs trembles in me,
What memory of immortal joy?

INTO WHAT PATTERN . . .

INTO what pattern, into what music have the spheres whirled us,
Of travelling light upon spindles of the stars wound us,
The great winds upon the hills and in hollows swirled us,
Into what currents the hollow waves and crested waters,
Molten veins of ancestral rock wrought us
In the caves, in the graves entangled the deep roots of us,

Into what vesture of memories earth layer upon layer enswathed us
Of the ever-changing faces and phases
Of the moon to be born, reborn, upborn, of sun-spun days
Our arrivals assigned us, our times and our places
Sanctuaries for all love's meetings and partings, departings
Healings and woundings and weepings and transfigurations?

UNSOLID MATTER

THESE bodies are of cloud so thin,
This tenuous vesture that we wear
Might pass through walls or worlds between
That mesh of fire, that mesh of air.

Oh could I travel on a thought
Through mountain's core and whelming waves
That break and drown and sweep apart
These bleeding selves that walk the ground!

Illusion all this seeming earth,
The wise may say; but strong the spell
That binds us fast to death and birth
And here and now, love's prison-cell.

IN MY SEVENTIETH YEAR

NOT lonely, now that I am old,
But still companioned like a child
Whose morning sun was friend enough,
And beauty of a field of flowers
Expressive as my mother's face.
So now, again, a tree in leaf,
Light falling on a London wall
Filtered through curtains or through leaves

Stirred in the gently moving air,
Or circles spreading in a pool
About each falling drop of rain,
A sparrow basking in the sun –
Each is the presence of the all,
And all things bear the signature
Of one unfathomable thought,
Lucid as universal light,
Music of innumerable
Voices of all living things
Together uttering one theme,
Voices of water, wind and bird,
The clear, familiar native speech
Of home, though seldom understood;
And I myself a spoken word,
Though ignorant of what I tell.

It is enough, now I am old,
That everywhere, above, beneath,
About, within me, is the one
Presence, more intimate and near
Than mothering hands or love's embrace.
All human love is strange and far
In comparison with this
Being more close than touch or breath,
Being that folds, enfolds, upholds
Me while I am; and since I am,
All being made me, brought me here,
Consubstantial with the earth,
Contemporaneous with the stars,
With the sun that lights the world,
Morning and night of the one day
In which I walk today, all days.

And since the utterance of the one
Majestic voice raised me to life
I am the part that I must play,
I am the journey I must go,
All that I am I must endure

And bear the burden of my years
Of good and evil, time and place,
Before the story all is told.
All that is possible must be
Before the concord can be full
Of earth's great cry of joy and woe.
Is this perhaps what men called God
Before the word lost meaning? This,
That needs no doctrine to make plain,
No cult to offer or withhold,
A union more intimate
Than breath of life, than flow of blood?
All creatures are the invited guests
At the unending wedding-feast
Of the one bridegroom, myriadfold
Engenderer of all that is.
Shall we condemn what he has made,
Who makes this world and calls it good,
Amends and heals through endless time?
All that I have done amiss,
All that I have failed to be,
Since he creates he must forgive,
Since he has made me he must love,
For I am but his act and will,
Who framed me both to give and bear
The wounds and sorrows of the world.

BOOK OF HOURS

BETWEEN the lines of earth's illuminated pages
Flash little garden birds from trees of green gold and red gold
Whose ornate branches bear
Perennial apple-harvest for hedgehog, snail and hare,
Holy grotesque animals of Paradisal field and sacred wood.
From vision-tinted skies

Sun, moon and stars their most rich hours rain down
On times and places of the book of life we mar.
The October guns are out after bronze plumage and golden eye,
Those azure hills, the silver-winding rivers
By us blasted and befouled. Yet still each day
Leaf after dreaming leaf new spaces of life unfold
Fit for the scripture of some legend other than the Fall
Of man and woman, and our violent ignorant deeds,
Bright ever-changing never-changing scene fit to adorn
Holy writ, heart's truth, prophetic wisdom.

A LOVE REMEMBERED

1

BEFORE we looked into each other's eyes
We were already
Travelling together on swift waves
Of light, and earth's sweet air
Breath of your breath and mine.
Voices of wind and water
Have uttered us from the beginning.
Timeless our meeting,
Of past and future all the now and here
Of many lives, the ever-blossoming tree.
I am old and alone, but boundless
All is everywhere,
Once is forever.

2

ONCE, as upon a living instrument attuned,
We seemed, at certain times,
The double vision of a single mind.
Images from dream to dream between us travelled:
A sparrow's flight, a blossoming rowan tree,

The wild song of a bird
Borne on the wind.
But after, other signs: a descending cloud,
A house on fire.

A skein of curlew
In fluent script across an evening sky
Of this world we had thought impervious to dreams
Traced your departure.
Grief wrote your message in the air, too thin
To veil its desolation. We knew, then,
I who live on, you in your hour of death,
That no dream is more tenuous than this
Flux of a seeming world that turns to memory
Where we can no more be, as once we were;
But memory returns to dream, transfigured
In regions of my sleeping or your waking,
Some poignant joy long past
Still trembling in the atmosphere of the heart,
A breath, a voice
Heard in another country, where, out of time, we meet.

3

Never for the first time
Love's meeting:
We know that we have known for ever
Each the other
Whose living eyes bring greeting
From the long forgotten.

Love the centre
Of a so great embrace,
Everywhere is here,
All time, all being
New in perpetual beginning,
Old as the stars.

And if before
This lifetime's fleeting

Does love know of after?
Are we not, even now,
Beyond death and parting
Still in that sphere?

4

I saw today a chain of geese fly over,
Underlit by the low winter sun
Their bodies gleaming, their great wings
Unflagging as they made for the Solway, your boyhood's shore.
You, like them, beyond sight
Were always departing,
I not the homecoming of your long flight
Whose heart beat with those beating wings' pure transit.
Here and now my woman's place,
Yours, always and only, elsewhere.

THE ORACLE IN THE HEART

The oracle in the heart
Spoke last night in deepest dream
One word: 'Regret'; then twice attempted,
An utterance more sound than word
But fraught with matter grave
Beyond articulation;
And yet who told must struggle to make known
That truth of the night,
Memory or foreknowledge not to be borne,
But someday must the unendurable all be told.

One other phrase clear among some withdrawn
From memory of the waking mind, or that, like Sibyl's leaves,
Wind-scattered, I failed to gather,
'Your life is trivial,' spoken plain. But whose the scorn

Pours on my centuries of days contempt of the immortal world?
Some better life, maybe,
I should or could have lived, and yet
The good and evil I have known and done
In measure as great as heart and mind can hold;
For one poor human life is like another,
Much beauty and much sorrow ours,
And ignorance more; yet, more or less, all tells
Of the one world one story. I have lived
A life and it suffices.
It seems the oracle must know
Some other world, some other mode
Of being on the other side of dream
That takes of lives like these
Little account; and yet this world,
Dark to the gods, how bright a paradise
When the heart loves, or when the mind forgets
Memory's load, year by year laid on us,
And welcomes, as if for the first time and for ever, the glad day.

BEHIND THE LIDS OF SLEEP

BEHIND the lids of sleep
In what clear river
Do the maimed, the misshapen
Bathe slender feet?
From what sky, what mountain
Do those waters pour
That wash away the stain
Of the world's mire?

On what journey
Does the night-traveller go
In quest of what lost treasure?
In what holy land

The mysteries shown,
Meaning beyond words or measure,
In what cave what ear of wheat?

Behind closed lids
The toil-worn stray
In fields not sown.
In childless arms a child is laid,
And, stilled with awe,
A bodiless mourner hears
A harmony too deep for senses dulled with pain.

By secret ways
The old revisit some long-vanished house
Once home, open a door
Where the long dead, made young again,
Offer the food of dream
That none may taste who would return.

Each to our own place
We go where none may follow
Nor hurt nor harm
The gentle wanderer whose waking days
Are exile, and whose slumbering form,
Vesture of soul clay cannot soil
Nor years deface,
Shabby and travel-worn.

APRIL 1976

FAMILIAR flowers:
In this cold April yet again
Crocus, tulip, daffodils
Of English gardens poets have praised
Since Skelton's, Shakespeare's, Marvell's days,
Where Hardy's milk-maids and Jane Austen's ladies,
Beatrix Potter's country-mice and gardeners' watering-cans

Have come and gone. Now it is I
Who in a darker year behold their Lenten beauty:
The same, or not the same? Have they
Too lost, with our human world, some purity
Of earlier times? Over their skies
Have drifted our foul clouds, our evil
Poisons earth, air and water. Do the lent-lilies know,
The garden blackbirds and the young daisies?

What is earth but the memory-trace of past ages
Woven into these intricate patterns, living forms
That tell of the creator and sustainer?
And of the destroyer does the garden know,
How the soft rain falls from tainted skies,
Seeps into root and blade,
And in the petals opening this spring day
The insidious harm already working its way
Into those delicate threads of life the spinners weave:
I sorrow for the flowers betrayed.

COLUMBINES

FINDING in a friend's garden columbines
It was as if they were those my mother grew,
And above all those coloured like a shell
Of rosy pearl seemed hers,
Returned, in all their freshness, from her garden
To remind me of, it should have been, happy days
When I was sheltered by her love and shared her flowers.
But by the vague bitter sorrow that arose
Out of the shadowy present of the past
I knew that it had not been so.
Wilful and unloving had been the daughter
My mother made, and all her flowers in vain
Offering her life to mine.
What did I hope to find when I turned away from her

Towards a cold future, now my sum of years,
From the unprized only love earth had for me,
Demeter's for her lost Persephone.

SUMMER GARDEN

Now, now and now
Northern sky over me,
Sun filtering through
Grey summer haze,
Swifts feeding high,
Two by two
Looping and diving,
Their new throats utter
Remembered voices.
In this old garden
Flowers bloom on
That my mother grew
And her mother before,
Sweet-williams and pansies,
The little white rose
The Jacobites wore.
Southernwood
And scent of briar
Spread on the evening
Memory of joy
That is always new.
Those sweet fore-mothers
Lived in this place
That has no ending,
These flowers were theirs,
This northern summer,
These swifts that fly
In fair weather high
In the delicate air.

Was their July
Milder than mine,
Their sky purer
Than over me now
As history darkens?
Were their hearts lighter,
Being innocent
Of what was to come
In the world I know?
Or is it I
Who for them see
This ageless beauty
Made anew
Because they hoped
For such a day
As I live now,
Because they gave,
Life after life,
The words of song
To a secret joy
That in them grew?

AH, GOD, I MAY NOT HATE . . .

Ah, God, I may not hate
Myself, who am your thought, who made
Earthworm and spider, gave
Being to the burying-beetle and the maggot,
Beak and talon and teeth, hunger to all creatures
Made to be your begetters and destroyers.
I who am living you from the numberless dead have raised
From the deathless dust of the grave
Dust of gleaming wings borne on the wind, seed
In the womb of the wind, borne
In cloud and tempest over the world

On tide and current made and unmade,
I am what you will, what you have willed
Life after life, maggot and spider, seed and harvest,
    chromosome, flame.

MY MOTHER'S BIRTHDAY

7 November 1880

I USED to watch you, sleeping,
Your once brown shining ringlets grey.
It was your way to lie,
Your knees high, your old twisted hands
In the archaic posture of the unborn,
Raised to your pillow, and I could see
How in the cradle you had lain
For comfort of your own warmth curled up
Like those poor children covered by the robin
With leaves, or under blanket of snow the snowdrop.
Your neglected childhood told its story
In the way you composed yourself for the grave.
Why had not your mother, bending over her baby,
Ninety years ago, wrapped you warm?
I, your daughter, felt pity
For that unwanted babe, for comfort too long ago, too
    far away.

SWEET-BRIAR FRAGRANCE...

SWEET-BRIAR fragrance on the air,
Late spring's forget-me-not, and early summer
Saxifrage and poppies, peonies and thyme,
Three young thrushes under the rhubarb leaves,

[255]

Broad beans in flower, pansies
Pricked out in boxes, too young for the border.
I have been alone; yet wish earth the better
Because of yet another summer my old eyes have seen
The beauty of this garden, the cattle grazing
Beyond the hawthorn hedge of my quiet acre.

RETURNING FROM CHURCH

THAT country spire – Samuel Palmer knew
What world they entered, who,
Kneeling in English village pew
Were near those angels whose golden effigies looked down
From Gothic vault or hammer-beam.
Grave sweet ancestral faces
Beheld, Sunday by Sunday, a holy place
Few find, who, pausing now
In empty churches, cannot guess
At those deep simple states of grace.

CAMPANULA

THIS morning, waking
But not yet remembering it was I
Who saw in my window white campanula stars
Against white mistiness
Curving like a shining hill upon the panes,
Remembered or discerned
A way of being those immaculate flowers
Were part of, once, some house
Of elegance and kindness, where I had been,
It seemed, or still remained, until the day
Opened the present and closed

That other time and place the flowers lingered in
A little longer than I. Another decade
It had been, or another life, whose ways
Were fine and clear as these
White visitants from a house of presences forgotten.

WINDS

I HAVE heard all day the voices
On the hills the loud winds
Utter from no place, clamour
Of bodies of air, speeding, whirling
Stream of invisible
Elements crying that are not,
Were, may be, living
The fields of the grass, lifting
Leaves of the forests, are not, have been, would be
Breath of all sentient beings, long lamentation
For living and loving and knowing, states of being
The wandering winds cannot
Discover for ever for all their seeking and wailing.

TOO MANY MEMORIES . . .

Too many memories confuse the old.
I call my grandson by my son's name –
Both laugh at me
Who so confuse identity,
So certain in the young, but I
See the one child returned from that place beyond time
Our children leave us for
When they turn men. I have known
Even myself pass,

And now my granddaughter is she
Who dreams undying dreams
And greets the high wind on the hills.

CANNA'S BASALT CRAGS

To their grey heights they rise,
The basalt crags thus far into blue air
Stayed where force into form no farther lifted
Archaic columns of fire frozen to stone
Temple where winds will sing, clouds gather
Till sun and ice of summers and winters totter
Their rocky hexagons. In vein and crevice
Wild bees find sweetness of wild thyme
Whose fine roots unfasten crystal by crystal, grain by grain
Boulders that tumble
Down slope whose stunted hazel leans to the prevailing weather.
Geometric unseen shapers limn
Wind-rounded water-worn contours of the isles
To the least lens winter-green moss turns to the sun
And bend of sedge a-quiver in current of air that lifts
Seabirds as rock-face turns gale from its course.
                                            What part in this
Concord of wisdom's unerring agents by whose design
Fall of farthest star by ever so little mountain and grass-blade stirs,
Sand-grain and rain-drop poised to fall
To the wet hill's trickling water-track, has a thought
That stays no tempest, leaves no trace
Of seer on seen, and yet knows all?

HOMAGE TO RUTLAND BOUGHTON

GREY shadow of old love forgotten,
Whence did these memories return
That, after five and fifty years,
Hearing last night a melody sung
That one long dead and I loved to,
It was as if the now of then
Was still young hearts' immortal hour,
Hearts once ours, though long grown cold,
His in the grave, mine in the world,
Whose seven-year body seven times
Time has replaced, that he desired
So long ago. Yet what is now
And what is time, where mortals are?
In soul's country first love's kiss
Beneath an apple-tree in flower,
Undying theme of music, once
Thought transient by youth, ourselves
Only the tremor of a sound
Heard as the timeless moves through time.

AS A HURT CHILD . . .

As a hurt child refuses comfort
We hide from one another, fearing to be hurt again
Should we give love or receive,
Vulnerable each time one small green shoot
Breaks through the hard wood
The years have ringed the heart with:
Where love, there pain.

WINIFRED'S GARDEN

For Winifred Nicholson

DEAR Bank's Head, in high summer overgrown
With garden-flowers run wild
And wild flowers chosen
Each for some beauty, to be a painter's friend
– Yellow Welsh poppy, Heart's Ease, Dusky Cranesbill
Woodruff and columbine –
I well remember when this tangle of flowers at ease,
Now song-birds' ambush, was a more tended place
Than now, when some new prize was set in place
That now blooms unregarded, or with a thought
Of in the autumn clearing to make room.
And yet your wise hand knows to spare,
Knows to let time weave on
Its tapestry of leaf and flower and song
Under your pearly northern sky.
We grow old, you and I, your garden
Dreams on its way from memory to sleep. Someday
All will be gone
But memories strewn like floating seed in many lives
Of such a day as this, and other days
Caught between the planned and the realised
Poised on the butterfly-wings of hovering paradise.

A VALENTINE

For John and Margaret Campbell

WARM behind curtains drawn to shut out February's cold,
About to play my embattled card
On the green baize, suddenly tears filled my eyes
To think that there will be a time
When the dear drawing-room of Canna House,

The owl-lamp on the Steinway grand, quartos
Of Schubert, Mozart, Celtic melodies,
The carved funny animals, the barque under glass,
The curious mirrors of carved bones
Made by French prisoners in Edinburgh castle,
Books on birds and minerals, cases of butterflies,
The family miniatures on ivory, piles
Of New Yorkers, Paris-Match, the Scotsman,
The friendly bottles, ash-trays, cigarettes,
The cat-clawed Chippendale and dog-haired cushions, photographs
Of Uist and Barra and of distant friends, all this
Learned happy accumulation, held together
By the presence of John and Margaret Campbell, by little dog
Patchen, successor to Perrita, sister of Cheekie of *The Western Isles*,
By Lobito, Freddie, Semolina and the other cats
Who step as lightly almost as memories
Of Mrs. Pink, Kukravat, Thomas Beattie, Reuben, Thoby and
      their friends,
Will be no more.
              Yet how can what is
Cease to be ever? Where in continuous time
Is moment divided from moment, that we should say
Is, was, will no more be?
What, if not ourselves, is memory
With all the known loved rooms where friends
Have come and gone? If soul
Be memory's place, where shall we look for one another
If not in these dear places still? I think of this
And other rooms and houses and gardens, and all
Cities and houses of the long past, their music and laughter,
And all the happy companionable things that gather
Where life is kind. How
Can all that here and now of then not be for ever?

A CANDLE-LIT ROOM

AN ancient house in the Marais,
Great carved portal, court, dark stairway
Little changed since Beaumarchais
Wrote, in that house, *Le Mariage de Figaro*.
We climbed as on the stair of years
To the room, candle-lit, where Mme Marcelle Jaujard
Keeps faith with a husband's memory,
Books, works of art, who saved for France
The paintings of the Louvre. (In the Resistance
There were those who risked death for such things.)
Those candle-flames deceived the sense of time,
Casting on old and on young faces
Shadows and likenesses
Of ancestors, known and unknown, old as France,
Portraits restored in flesh and blood,
Still bearing the old names: de Margerie,
De la Rochefoucauld, de Chabonne La Palice,
Yves, Diane, François-Xavier, Jean,
Poet, young musician, painter, Jesuit,
The fair Russian émigrée who truly said
(Though she had not) 'I have met you before'
Actress who in the Comédie Française had played the
        famous parts –
All practising the old arts that draw spirits like moths
Out of the night to celebrate
That human mystery all arts praise.

I was the stranger who came with news
Of another country, old as France, invisible neighbouring land
Whose words I have inherited as they faces and names,
Words, like names and faces, long handed down,
Mine for a time, to relinquish and pass on
To others who may gather in that room or other rooms,
Their features briefly lit by the undying flame.

SHORT POEMS

What does this day bestow?
Beauty of sparse snow
Whose wet flakes touch
The soil, then vanish.

*

Frost-rime edges blades of grass,
The garden blackbird crosses
The motionless air
To the rigid hawthorn.

*

London air dims
Blue of a cold spring sky,
Bricks as usual, and the morning news;
But rook and robin tell other things.

*

Moon golden towards the full,
Summits of pine afloat
Over level mist, the hills
Cloudlike, adrift.

*

I drink with my eyes a sphere
Charged with light, of rain
On tip of briar
Rose-leaf posed
To fall, tinctured with green.

*

These I name: swallow, hawthorn, rain:
But meaning traces its bird
Swift between grey and green
Mystery unbound by word.

THESE watery diamond spheres
Fall, quench in soil
Thirst of all dead who toil
In Hades' house, where roots
Drink from the skies.

*

ON its way I see
The anew-created
Garden as old as woman; to me
These daisies in the grass are shown, these
Birds in the apple-tree:
Is my sin, then,
Forgiven?

*

FOREST is multitude,
But one tree all, one apple-bud
Opens the flower of the world, infinite
Golden stamens and rose petals, here.

*

AH, many, many are the dead
Who hold this pen and with my fingers write:
What am I but their memory
Whose afterlife I live, who haunt
My waking and my sleep with the untold?

*

MY sight with the clouds'
Unimpeded rest in changing moves
Across the sky: the aged in endless
Unbecoming are at peace.

*

ALL the garden
In this uncrumpled yellow poppy
Of whose uncounted anthers' countless pollen –
Life's infinity.

*

I COULD have told much by the way
But having reached this quiet place can say
Only that old joy and pain mean less
Than these green garden buds
The wind stirs gently.

*

UNDER these hills too high and bare
For love or war
I live in a green place without a story:
Sun, cloud, wind; beyond
My gate the simple fields that Adam tilled.

*

FROM vague regions of sleep I come again
To a cottage in a green field, flowers
Many-coloured, wind, sky, stability of day.
Do the dead, in dreams astray
Seek in vain the gate that opens
Into this world each morning?

*

IN the high lonely hills
Long ago astray: why
Did the great merciless winds
Fill my heart with joy?

*

WHAT have I to regret
Who, being old,
Have forgotten who I am?
I have known much in my time
But now behold
Procession of slow clouds across my sky.

*

THIS little house
No smaller than the world
Nor I lonely
Dwelling in all that is.

*

YOUNG or old
What was I but a story told
By an unageing one?

*

TODAY as I
Looked up at the sky's great face
I saw the bright heavens gaze
Down upon me.

*

IF, into this evening as the grass receives the dew
I could step out of myself on weightless feet
I would be with the grass-blades, the dew-gatherers,
But cannot cross
The frontiers of their green kingdom cool and still
In my dense body,
Walking this twilit grass towards the grave.

*

LAST night I seemed in your embrace,
And sorrowing because you were about to die
Pleaded with you from my soul
Soul's immortality. Today
I wake into my place,
You beyond death, I mortal.

*

DEAR ones in the house of the dead,
Can you forgive
An old woman who was your proud
Daughter, who now too late
Returns your love?

*

WHEN I woke to the snow
Joy for a moment stirred in me:
Happy expectation of a Christmas-tree
Long ago.

*

SIX calices yellow gold,
Fire-gold one, seven
Lamps of the Almighty, flame
Today in my garden, blown
Poppies in the wind:
In the beginning kindled they
Burn on.

*

FLOWER, memory –
My old eyes behold
Late narcissus' green-gold pheasant's eye,
Petals fresh pleated; scent
Immemorial. Now
Is all my springs'
Sorrow, joy.

*

JUNE day, grey
Sky, north wind sighs
Ceaseless sorrowless
Breath of spacious sky
Shaking the long grass, the apple-petals
Blowing away.

*

LIFELONG ago such days
Of travelling cloud and ceaseless wind
Sealed my flesh and blood
Native of wild hills.
Elsewhere sun and summer, here
High elementals of the air.

*

TODAY:
This leafy apple-tree, grey
And gentle sky where the winds stray
Among mothering clouds, soft
Breast where every thirst
Cools its burning, rests in changing
Mist and air, light.

*

I've read all the books but one
Only remains sacred: this
Volume of wonders, open
Always before my eyes.

*

Who shows me this scene?
Mother who made me, your past is hidden
From me, who am your present, and receive
The unbeginning unending
Now of rain falling on spring grass,
On stone, on leaf.

*

I asked not for the good
But for the beauty of the world:
In every gleam of light,
Of opening leaves,
Of living wings and eyes, uncounted multitude
Of the aspects of God,
Lifelong, in what abundance given.

*

To sight sky seems
At times a place where soul may walk
Earth's cloudy hills, may climb
From world to world.

*

Soul travels far and far
Until the worlds are one another;
Substance shadow
Falling on purest mirroring seas, images
What elsewhere is.

*

WORLD:
Image on water, waves
Break and it is gone, yet
It was.

*

THE curlew knew today
Advent of spring; they
Cry their wild cry
Whose human word is joy.

*

SOFT, soft sound of wings
In multitude, starlings
Low over my house pass.

FROM

The Presence

(1987)

A DEPARTURE

1

Always and only in the present, the garden,
Always today of past and future the sum,

Endless everlasting light in flower
In flowers and leaves, in boundless sky pure.

East of the westering sun, west of the new moon
Stands my small northern house and daffodils in bloom,

Yet in this wide beautiful eternal place
My heart is sore with memories and loss,

For I am leaving you, my little world,
That still today shines with the golden light,

End and beginning of the one epiphany
Here and now of all that was, all that will be.

Grief, departure, exile – what are these
Mute Eumenides, who for all the bird-song and the daisies
Compel from my reluctant eyes these futile tears?

2

'Be glad' (a far voice speaks to me)
'Be glad you are required to part
From all that withholds you from being free
As the hills, as the clouds, as bird and tree.
Break all bonds, old woman, while you may,
Enter your own eternity.'

'Then what is grief?' I reply,
'Unriddle me this sore heart
That has no words, but tells and tells
From mother to daughter, daughter to mother
That love must choose, over and over,

Mortal things, all earth's minute
Petals and wings.'

'You have loved other gardens long ago,
And all in the one green veil are woven together,
Unbroken the stream of the light, the stream of the air,
Seed to grass, acorn to oak, forest to fire,
The unborn and the dead companion you everywhere,
Where you have been always, you are.'

'It is their transience makes dear
Places and days that once were home,
Sheltering refuges of earth
Nearest at heart when they are gone,
Faces we do not see again;
Is it not death that seals our love?'

3

It winds into the heart,
That unbroken thread
From present to past,
Without to within,
From seen to seer,
Sky, garden, tree, bird
Transmuted, transposed
To memory, to pain
These young leaves, these daisies,
The dappling wind
That glances on blades
Of glistering grass,
Become what I am
Who am the sum
Of all I have lost,
Who am the maker,
From greenness a joy,
From wind, wisdom,
From cold earth, gold,
From gold of the sun

Life-blood of sorrow
That sounds the heart.
I am my past
And future approaching
Days unknown.

But of all these none
Brighter nor dearer
Than the wind and the daisies,
The little hedge-sparrow
Fearless and sun-glossed
Searching the flower-bed
Outside my window,
Winged with time
The ever-present
Flitting and flaunting
Its here and now
Light into love,
Leaf into loss.

4

VISTA of winter woods where we will go no more –
The frozen lake, mute swans; beyond,
That château all remember
Where dwells, or where once dwelt –
I glimpsed, long, long ago, the place, but they are dead to us
Who in another time, another land
Are what we might have been, might be
If world were reverie, or dream a world.

The two black watch-dogs guard;
Propitiatory cake to close those mouths –
Hope out of what memory
Like music in still air, as if – but here
The dream is changed: no door into that house.

INTO this meagre earth, all these last years,
Imagined paradise has in these budding apple-trees,
These daisies closing in the evening grass,
Sent down invisible roots
That now I must tear up again,
From this little house wrench its inhabiting dream.

This quiet room –
Oak cupboard, lamp, the jug of daffodils,
The little bunch of wood anemones
Left by my granddaughter who herself is gone,
This sheltering present only another memory-place
Where loved ghosts wander,
Who are ourselves grown tenuous
Haunters of home we can never re-enter.

My mother's arm-chair, the writing-desk where my father
Kept faded snapshots, his sister's bible, my grandfather's last letter;
Painting of a rainbow a friend made from this very window,
The cups and plates, the dominos and jigsaw-puzzles,
The cat hearth-rug and faded Morris curtains
Never again together.
Moss and sticks do not make a nest, but the careful weaver
Of fragments the winter winds will scatter.

Logs glow on the hearth, the evening sky is clear
In the west where the sun has set, darker
Where the rising moon, one day past Easter,
Is veiled in cloud. Snipe whirr
Over the marsh: it seems that never
Could I let go this here and now;
But on my unsteady table yet again I write in sorrow:

Eternity's long now is for us unending departure.

6

THIS, my last home
Is woven of memories
Lifelong; my mother's
Bridal-gifts, linen
Her fingers sewed,
Her work-table stored
With thimble and skein.
I have lived on
In my mother's world
With things her fingers
Endeared by touch,
Cake-tins, kitchen gear
Tell of her life,
Of hearth and table
Swept and spread
For husband and child,
Silent messengers
Charged with her love
To be delivered
Now she is gone
Who from her dreams
Drew out each clue
To be unwound,
Each stitch a thought
To clothe, to hold fast
Her one daughter
Someday in a future
That is now my past.

It is myself
I leave behind,
My mother's child,
Simple, unlearned,
Whose soul's country
Was these bright hills,
This northern sky.

7

TAKE but a step
And there is no return,
Look back from the field gate,
Home is already gone.

'I could have changed my mind' –
But the one mind knows all
Future and past together
In the unchanging whole.

'What if some other way
The price were found
I need to keep this house,
Could I not then stay?

What is the sum I need
But loaves and fishes multiplied?'
But even he
Whose hands bestowed

Harvest of earth and sea
Knew when his time had come,
Might not evade
By the mere turning of an ass's head

What he had to do,
Although he chose
Of all the directions of the world
The worst road.

8

WHAT, then, do they gain
Who follow an invisible master,
Leave home, wife, father and mother?
Nothing! Who can bargain
With that giver who takes all?
But being what we are, must travel;
Who are ourselves his way unknown,
His untold truth, his light unseen.

IN PARALDA'S KINGDOM

1

ALL day I have listened to their voices sounding
Over the high fells, the wind's kingdom,
Unhindered elementals of the air,
Their long continuous word meaning
Neither sorrow nor joy, loud singing
Great angels of the stars will hear when I am gone.

2

AT rest in changing:
Across the blue they move
Passive in the embrace of the winds of heaven,
Visible melting into invisible, to reappear
In wisp and fringe of pure
Vapour of whitest mist as slowly they gather and come together
In serene for ever
Unbroken commingling consummation of water and air.

3

THEY accuse none,
Rays of the westering sun, or these
Folding clover leaves and sleeping daisies,
The missel-thrush that sings
To me, to all within the compass of his song,
My neighbour field-mouse
Venturing tremulous from hide under stone
Accepts the crumbs I have scattered;
From grass-blade to farthest star nothing withheld
From the unjust or the just; whom also made
The giver of these.

4

SWIFT cloud streaming over the northern hill,
One moment dark, then vanishing
To rise in pulsing multitude
Of wings, turning again, returning, pouring
In current of invisible wind, condensing
In black core, to burst again
In smoke of flight windborne, upborne
Dust moved by will
Of single soul in joy innumerable, and I
The watcher rise with the rising, pour with the descending
Cloud of the living, read in the evening sky
The unending word they spell, delight.

LONG ago, over the Northumbrian moors, as I lay safe in bed
I heard the elemental host
On chariot clouds riding the wings of the wind.
Framed text on my bedroom wall in daylight read
'Children obey your parents in the Lord,
For this is right'; but in the outer night
Unborn undying voices instructed me:
'You were with us before you entered that warm womb,
Free as we are free; none tells
The wind how it should blow, the stars their courses.'
                                                    And I,

A child remembering that anterior state
Communed with them; and still I hear them
Uttering a wisdom I have lost over the bare hills.

STILLNESS after storm, heart at rest
In quiet song
Of missel-thrush; the winds
Have fallen, their work done.

I who am of another kingdom
Yet have endured their blast,
Attended their wisdom,
My work too ended,

Who to their wild voices
Have added my descant
Of joy and sorrow,
Sounding of intangible thought.

Who made that music
Alone can know
What meaning moves
When gale winds from the hills blow.

7

ON wet west wind soft sift of rain
Wafts from birch and briar breath
Of invisible life on the invisible air:
From memory's lost beginning
Recollection from beyond time reminds that love
Is for nothing other,
But a state of being
            long forgotten.

LIGHT OVER WATER

BRILLIANT
Myriad instantaneous alighting raindrops on a stream
That has run unbroken down and on
Since this once familiar place was home,

Each in its alighting flashes sun's glitter and is gone
As another, and another and another come to meet me,
Angel after angel after angel, its dancing-point
Always here and now,
The same bright innumerable company arriving,
Anew the present always absolving from time's flow.

Old, I know
How many, many, many the epiphanies of light.

*

And yet now as I write
They are only memories,
Those bright arrivals of the travelling light,
Now nowhere, never again.
No road or bridge or gate
Into the past, once now, once here,
Nor farthest star comes near
Where they are gone, who once were dear;
For memory is Hades' house
Where none is present, where none meet.

*

And yet again, always
Those presences come to us, are seen, are known,
Messengers of meaning, sacred, indecipherable,
Present everywhere, to all.
Inaccessible as life their source;
We know untold, untaught
Who they are, what holy truth proclaim.
The knower a mystery, a mystery the known,
Forms of wisdom in perpetual epiphany, they and we,
Sun and eye, seer and seen,
Daily angels, sun and stars, river and rain.

MIMOSA-SPRAY

My dear mother
One mimosa-spray
Long ago, from an imagined Italy
She would never see
Offered her daughter
From a far-off blossoming tree.

Today
In a mimosa-grove
Heavy with flower-gold dust
I met in memory
My mother on that day
When I turned from her
Love's simplicity.

I who have rifled the world's beauty
Now will never enter
That golden garden she offered me.

A SMALL MATTER...

A SMALL matter
Whether I hope
To be blessed, or despair
With the lost, on the last
Or any day.

Enough to be
Part and particle
Of the whole
Wonder and scope
Of this glory.

Cannot even
The condemned rejoice
That the Presence
Is, and is just?

[283]

WORLD'S MUSIC CHANGES ...

WORLD'S music changes:
The spheres no longer sing to us
Those harmonies
That raised cathedral arches,
Walls of cities.

Soundings of chaos
Dislodge the keystone of our dreams,
Built high, laid low:
Hearing, we echo
Rumours of the abyss.

There was a time
To build those cloud-capped towers,
Imagined palaces, heavenly houses,
But a new age brings
A time to undo, to unknow.

TELL ME, DARK WORLD ...

TELL me, dark world,
What it is you know
That I dare not.

Destruction is the mode,
Love an old story
That none believes.

I ask the grass:
To every living cell
God's secret told,

Knowledge of the all,
In each seed
The axis mundi

Where blood is shed
Of one who dies
And rises from the dead.

I HAD MEANT TO WRITE . . .

I HAD meant to write a different poem,
But, pausing for a moment in my unweeded garden,
Noticed, all at once, paradise descending in the morning sun
Filtered through leaves,
Enlightening the meagre London ground, touching with green
Transparency the cells of life.
The blackbird hopped down, robin and sparrow came,
And the thrush, whose nest is hidden
Somewhere, it must be, among invading buildings
Whose walls close in,
But for the garden birds inexhaustible living waters
Fill a stone basin from a garden hose.

I think, it will soon be time
To return to the house, to the day's occupation,
But here, time neither comes nor goes.
The birds do not hurry away, their day
Neither begins nor ends.
Why can I not stay? Why leave
Here, where it is always,
And time leads only away
From this hidden ever-present simple place.

THE FORE-MOTHER

I AM spread wide, far
On the tide of the one sea,
As I ebb away
In lives not mine
My blood flows on.

Like a mist lifting
I fade,
I no longer am
Who through new eyes see
The green, the vein,
The flower, the tree.

I am an echo
You do not hear,
Who, gone from myself,
Am near
Your here and now
Of elsewhere.

I am long ago
Who am with you.
In your first love
Age-old, the untold
I speak to you.

LILY OF THE VALLEY

No, it is not different,
Now I am old,
The meaning and promise
Of a fragrance that told
Of love to come
To the young and beautiful:
Still it tells

The unageing soul
All that heart desires
For ever is
Its own bliss.

THE PRESENCE

PRESENT, ever-present presence,
Never have you not been
Here and now in every now and here,
And still you bring
From your treasury of colour, of light,
Of scents, of notes, the evening blackbird's song,
How clear among the green and fragrant leaves,
As in childhood always new, anew.
My hand that writes is ageing, but I too
Repeat only and again
The one human song, from memory
Of a joy, a mode
Not I but the music knows
That forms, informs us, utters with our voices
Concord of heaven and earth, of high and low, who are
That music of the spheres Pythagoras heard.
I, living, utter as the blackbird
In ignorance of what it tells, the undying voice.

THREADING MY WAY . . .

THREADING my way, devious in its weaving
Into the web of the world,
Time's warp running from far back, and on
Of lives, crossed life-lines, intercrossed, entangled,
Knotted, knitted together, ravelled, unravelled,

Hidden, re-emerging in new design,
Always growing, unseen or seen
Patterns we make with one another, distant
Or near, from immemorial past
Into unbounded future running unbroken,
Threads so fine and subtle of lives
We weave and interweave, slender as light,
Intangible substance of the age-old
Ever-extending all, makers and made
Who feel the pull of love, of grief, on every thread.

WOODRUFF

Today the Presence
Has set before me
Woodruff's white foam
Of petals immaculate,
Fourfold stars numberless
Open life's centres,
In a London garden
They grow in a spring wood
Before the city and after
Machines whose noise
Tears the sky.
The white stars
Do not hear; they tell me
'The woods are always.'
Lily of the valley
Feels for loam of leaves
And the blackbirds
Build anew, repair
The rents we tear
In times and places.
Immemorial woods
Are here, are near,
The white stars cross

The invisible frontier:
'Come to us,' the flowers say,
'We will show you the way.'

SAY ALL IS ILLUSION ...

SAY all is illusion,
Yet that nothing all
This inexhaustible
Treasury of seeming,
The blackbird singing,
The rain coming on,
The leaves green,
The rainbow appearing,
Reality or dream
What difference? I have seen.

THAT FLASH OF JOY ...

THAT flash of joy –
Mine, or another's or from elsewhere, far
Like scent of budding leaves borne on the wind,
Or pure note, clear,
Heart trembles to, like water in a glass,
Like a flame that bows and leaps
As sound-waves pass,
Poignant as first love remembered,
The past, the lost, the never-to-be
Glimpsed between the coming and the gone.
It seemed a room that I had lived in once
And found again just as it was,
But where that country out of time?
Was that recollection mine,
Or being itself, life in all its sweetness
Known for a moment, understood.

[289]

CHANGE

Change
Said the sun to the moon,
You cannot stay.

Change
Says moon to the waters,
All is flowing.

Change
Says the field to the grass,
Seed-time and harvest,
Chaff and grain.

You must change,
Said the worm to the bud,
Though not to a rose,

Petals fade
That wings may rise
Borne on the wind.

You are changing,
Said death to the maiden, your wan face
To memory, to beauty.

Are you ready to change?
Says thought to the heart, to let pass
All your lifelong

For the unknown, the unborn
In the alchemy
Of the world's dream?

You will change,
Say the stars to the sun,
Says night to the stars.

NAMED

In a dream, a voice
Called me by my name,
Unknown, or known from some far other time
Or place or state or world, yet nearer
Than here and now, that hidden one;
And was it I,
Unselved by sleep that takes away
All daily doing and being,
Absolved for a space from what we are, or seem,
Am I, who remember,
Another, or the same
Who stirred,
Who answered to my name
Recalled from lifelong years away, astray,
Forgetful and forgotten, since I had been
One named?
        Strange among strangers my face,
Defaced, obscured, obliterate,
Falsified by the years, disguised,
Anonymous, who, when addressed,
Some other, or no-one;

Yet by that unknown knower I am known
And who I am.

AN OLD STORY

1

I was in a garden
Where the trees flower,
Where birds sing
And waters run,

But my mind wandered
For a moment only
Of life-long time
I was astray,

A life-time gone –
But where are they,
The dazzling waters,
The creatures at play?

Still I see
White clouds, bright sun,
I touch young leaves,
Breathe the wild rose,

But they are far
As love from loss,
As come from gone.

2

THIS was not what I meant,
My life amiss

From day to day
How did I lose my way
From moment to moment?

The hours run on
Through the unkind act,
The lifelong loss,

But what is done
Long outlasts
Deed and doer,

There is no end,
From life to life
We repair what we can.

I have done what I am,
Am what I have done,
Yet meant far other.

3

READER, I would tell
If I knew
That all shall be well,

All darkness gone,
All lives made whole,
Hearts healed that were broken,

Would tell of joy reborn,
Of wrongs made right,
Of harms forgiven,

But do not know
How what is done
Can ever not be,

Though love would wish it so.

4

WHO so well as the lost
Can know, from absence,
Who better, so far removed,
Measure by want love's fullness?
Of that kindness
In which a myriad creatures live in peace,
I, who know evil and good
Ask no mercy, yet
Claim as by right
Best right to praise.

BLUE COLUMBINES

For Jeremy

ALIGHT with dark
Fire, mystery
Kindled from seed to seed,
Garden to garden, spring to spring
Indigo
Darkness illuminate
Flaring at noon, colour of night-sky
Of the seven rays deepest
Solemnity of blue cathedral glory
Of womb, secret of shade,
Ablaze in my last garden, profound
Sounding of the afar, the beyond.

NATARAJA

1

TIME, rhythm
Of forms that open,
Forms that pass,

Perfect or marred,
The foot of the God
Is on the world,

Terrible dancer
Whose trampling tread
Crushes evil and good,

The flow of his river
Is in our blood,

End and beginning,
A beat of the heart
Our all, our nothing.

Destroyer of worlds,
The purifier,
His step indifferent,
His garment red.

2

How else
But by that trampling foot
Can be effaced
Our nightmare cities,
The dead-ends, the maze,
The culs-de-sac,
The locked rooms, the windowless
Prisons, the closed minds,
The entrenched positions,
The safes, the cellars,
The death-proof shelters,
The high-rise towers of loneliness?

Who else
But the world-destroyer
Can free us from this state
And place of no return,
The inescapable consequence,
Impasse, end of the road.
We, fallen, can fall
No farther, hopes and fears
Converge in this
Term of what's done,
Thought, word and deed here end
In entropy. There is nowhere to run.

I, who have become
What I am,
Am what I have done,
Free-will has come to this.
Back to the wall
I speak for all

Who, at bay,
Stand in extremis:
Only that Power can
Who will destroy us, free us.

Obliterate our trace, the fire,
The purifier!

NAMELESS ROSE

SOMETIME, some where
Always I hoped to find again
The rose whose trusses of pearl-
Shell-petalled flowers
Climbed to my first window-sill.
My mother did not know its name.

Some where, some time
That flourishing tree, whose buds, sun-warm
Opened gold-stemmed on the wall
Centres of sweet small roses
Whose petals fell too soon
I hoped to find,

But in no catalogue, no visited garden
My mother's nameless rose, until
Today in Italy, where summer
In multitude is blooming,
By a ruined wall I came
Upon a bower, and did not dare

To look too close, fearing to find
That rose too a stranger, yet
When I came near, each shell-pearl petal
Slipped into memory's place:
'Look, we are here,' they told me, 'then
Is now again.' Almost

I believed them, for they were the same
As in those childhood summers past,
Those withered petals made anew;
But I was not, for years between,
Tears and estrangement, my mother's sorrow
No flowers could comfort, nor mine now.

THE INVISIBLE KINGDOM

WE know more than we know
Who see always the bewildering proliferating
Multiplicity of the common show.

There come to the artist's hands
Such subtleties of form, of light,
Gardens, presences,

Faces so tenderly beautiful
We wonder with what untaught knowledge seen,
Beyond the commonplace the hidden

Aspects of mystery, secrets
Known only to the soul,
Known only to love, immeasurable

Wisdom from our own hands' work grown,
Expression of a knowledge not our own
Which yet guides brush and pen, obedient

To an omniscience we, though ignorant, yet share
Whose hearts respond and answer
To Schubert's music, and Mozart's, they knowing no more

Than we of the celestial harmonies
They heard above the continual dissonance
The immediate imposes.

Yet unceasing
The music of the spheres, the *magia* of light,
Spirit's self-knowledge in its flow

Imaging continually the all
Of which each moment is the presence
Telling itself to the listener, the seer in the heart

Contemplates in time's river
The ever-changing never-changing face.

STORY'S END

O, I would tell soul's story to the end,
Psyche on bruised feet walking the hard ways,
The knives, the mountain of ice,
Seeking her beloved through all the world,
Remembering – until at last she knows
Only that long ago she set out to find –
But whom or in what place
No longer has a name.
So through life's long years she stumbles on
From habit enduring all. Clouds
Disintegrate in sky's emptiness.
She who once loved remembers only that once she loved:
Is it I who wrote this?

HONESTY

Too long astray –
Time, from hour to hour,
Lifelong, unending departure –

In my withering garden
A country flower,
'Honesty', prized for its signature,

Because, its seeds set,
Fall from a clear membrane,
Emblem of pure intent.

I thought to have come indoors
Not to this room
But to another, as it was,

Honesty and dried grass
In an alabaster vase,
Lamp alight, curtains drawn
Against the night –

Childhood, the holy day –
A moment, a turning away,
And never again.

H.G.A.

Too long away,
You have drawn near, of late,
Or is it I,
Late, who return,
Nearing my end of time,
To your timeless place?
I have lived lifelong
My works and days with friends and strangers,
Now those ties
I and they have woven
No longer bind me, alone,
Duties, done or undone, forgotten.
How easily a lifetime falls away
And I stand free,
Now, again, as then.
Invisible companion ever young,
Lead me away
Where you will, beyond memories,
Beyond past days and vanished houses,
Remembered and forgotten faces.
Here is not my place, nor I this.

A DREAM

THOSE birds of dream,
Circling high as eagles the skies of sleep,
Descending to rest in trees —
I saw with wonder birds of paradise,
Rainbow-hued, luminous
Their plumage, and others grey as doves.
Again into that inner sky they rose, but then
Returned once more to await. Are these
Birds of soul's country images
Of earth, remembered? Peacocks
Adorning miniatures of Brindavan, or Persian pages
Painted with two squirrel-hairs by craftsmen
Skilled in marvels,
Are they of inner or of outer skies,
Nature's splendour, or memory's?
Or are earth's peacocks' jewelled ocelli
Mirrors of paradise? Their plumes
That make the light shimmer are only dust
Of the earth, their lustre in the beholder's eye.
Where, of what land are they?
Or when did dust and spirit
So separate that creatures of clay
Ceased to mean heaven,
The birds of heaven fly from our waking world away?

JESSIE

A COUSIN sent it me,
Found in the back of a drawer,
A broken brooch engraved with my mother's name,
Returned from long ago, when I
Knew by heart those silver clover-leaves and flowers
Small as forget-me-nots.

Then they were part of the known, whole world
My mother gave me; her name a message whose simple meaning
Is herself, once dear and familiar, now dear and far.

WHO ARE WE?

NOT that I remember, but that I am
Memory, am all that has befallen
Unbroken being and knowing
Whose flow has brought me here, laden with the forgotten
Times and places, once here and now
Of those who were, from day to day,
From life to life, as I,
Presences of that omnipresence without end or beginning,
Omniscient through our being,
That brings and takes away the unremembered living
Moments of joy and wisdom, the once-familiar
Rooms and temples and fountains, the long-ago gardens
Of a thousand summers, music once heard,
Travelling through me and on, like a wave
Of sound, a gleam
Irrecapturable. And who are we
Who gather each one leaf, one life of the myriadfold tree
Of the lost domain, and mourn
The flowing away of all we never were, or knew?
Promises, messages reach us, instruct us,
The untold, the untellable, undying
Heart's desire, resonance
Of elsewhere, once, some day, for ever.

A CANDLE FOR ALL SAINTS, ALL SOULS

For Antonia – whom I haven't met.

In this book, gift of an unknown friend
Hoping I might find words to kindle
Some illumination of mind or heart,
There remain many spacious pages where I still
May trace life's record, as the ant in dust,
The beetle under elm-bark, the snail
Its lustrous trail, or track of hare on the bare snow.
All leave their signature, as skeleton veins
Record spring's sap-flow in leaves once green.
What the pattern, what the meaning, these toilers know
Not more than I what or to whom I tell –
No more than the small house-fly that alights
Now on this page, whose script
Only the writer of the book of life can read.

On my shelves closed books of many lives,
Knowledge of the long dead, who lived these thoughts.
I have explored their regions of wisdom and wonder,
As others will relive their ever-present past
Whose records, written or unwritten, remembered or forgotten
Come to us in words spoken by living lips
Of the wise and the unwise, long-ago voices repeating
The never-ending stories of the loved and known
As being moves through every here and now, delighting
In all we have been and seen and done, endured,
Imagined and dreamed.
Fragments, traces remain, perfect like fossil shells,
Pages unfaded, painted walls, or sculptured stone,
Writings on bark or palm-leaves, scripts
Decipherable still by some, though few
Who from old manuscripts can rekindle the light
That once illumined texts of treasured wisdom
Transcribed by monks of Kells or Nalanda.
The gods themselves told the creation-stories
To those first ancestors whose scriptures were the stars

Who knew the speech of insect and bird, of rock and cloud,
The innumerable living, each a universe
Boundless in its own presence,
Undying in the imagination of the world.
I leave my trace, with theirs, in timelessness.

LONDON RAIN

THESE diamond spheres
Tainted from poisoned air that blows about the houses,
Each sour raindrop hanging from wire or railings
Yet catches its ray to open the rainbow light
Of heavenly promise before it falls
On sterile ground to moisten the patient moss
That mends with living green
Of Paradise, springing from blown dust in cracks and crevices
For lonely downcast eyes to find a long-ago familiar place.

LONDON WIND

WIND, lifting litter, paper, empty containers, grit,
Even here blows the element of air –
Between post-office and supermarket still the caress
Of earth's breath cool on my face
As gusts in spirals and eddies whirl
Spent leaves from London's plane-trees, to let fall
Perfect forms so lightly poised on a vandalized lot.

WISDOM OF WORDS

Through this pen-point, this punctum
These old fingers inscribe my intricate line
Of words, beyond-price heritage from those
Who speak in soundless, loved, remembered voices
Of multitudes who in world's without-end times and places
Each in their once-and-for-ever here and now remains.

Sisters and brothers of dust, whose faces
I have never seen, young and beautiful, learned
Or wise, whose words have told
And tell me all your hearts have known,
Your long-ago loves are with me now and always
Who breathe the unbounded air that carries your far voices.

From word to word I trace my way, seeking, divining
Scarcely discernible messages, passing
From life to life clarities, marvels, epiphanies
All hearts, all souls have sought,
Bringing to my moment all those who once were, have dreamed,
Have known and praised, have sung, have cried aloud.

Cosmic music of water and wind and stars
Flows on for ever, but this human realm
Of meaning, none knows but we,
These memories, told and retold, imparted
From dream to dreamer by such as I,
Whose only knowledge is what we have made to be.

FROM
Living With Mystery
(1992)

HYMN TO TIME

1

TIME, taker away of all that is,
   Your river flows always through our days
Continuous, unbroken, mirroring surface
That holds no trace
Of us, as that invisible flow passes and passes:
We rest in changing, who are now always.
Unending Time takes away and brings
World's hourly beauty, the rich days,
All I have seen, countries and seas and cities,
Meetings of minds, laughter and wisdom and kindness,
Where have you gone, mountain streams and shell-strewn beaches
Where now was once?
A week ago, now was Paris, dear French friends,
Was the Luxembourg gardens, where the orange-trees
Were being wheeled away for another winter, and now
Was first sixty years ago under those chestnut shades –
How smoothly, Time, you conjure away our times and places!

Time, taker away of all loved things
That were here, that were home,
When did you take, and where, the once and never again?
Now was a stone cottage under Tindale Fell,
The wrens' nest, and Sweet Williams, and apple-trees,
Was scrabble with Christina by her wood fire, her dogs
Snoring on the sofa, was the scent of Winifred's oil-paints,
Was College rooms in Girton, was a London bomb-shelter,
Was my father correcting exercise books, I doing difficult sums
On the blue serge cloth of the dining-room table,
Now was the fragrance of a Maiden's Blush rose
In my mother's garden, lilac and pinks and pansies,
Was the Manse kitchen where the clock on the wall
Ticked away the quiet hours
Till bedtime and the storm blowing round the house,

Was looking up at the cold winter stars.
Now without end or beginning Time
With your long necklace of skulls, who will add mine
To your tally of lives, each rich in its infinite present,
Nothing, take as you will all that was once ours
As from moment to moment, day to day
All that for ever is passes before us,
Will ever not have been once and for ever.

2

TIME, kind taker-away
Of sorrow, whose now is unending,
Grief to whose pain I clung
As a last link with one gone,

On what day, unnoticed Time,
Did I forget to remember? To become
Another one than that desolate woman
Weeping by a dark stream?

The moment is eternal of love, of pain,
But eternal moments pass –
My hair is grey, kind Time,
Old loves, old sorrows, no longer mine.

Unwillingly I all I once desired
Relinquished, and reluctantly
Let go what I could not hold –
How rich time's treasury
With our past loves!

3

TIME, I have bathed my feet in your sacred river, whose stream
Flows pure from the mountains to the sea. Waking, I have seen
As in a dream where all is meaning,
Ganges come down from the heights where the gods dwell

Above the clouds, and the sound of waters
Where rishis tell their beads gathered from forest trees
To the human places where boats ply on the abundant flow,
Men and women and children, laughter, shoals of fish below.
Down by the river-side beggars and lepers in the sun
Who gives life to the living and to the dying darkness,
India! where life's a dream
Of profound untellable mysteries.

Living river, whose swift waters are worshipped as the sun sets
In your ancient holy city where the gods show themselves
As in every temple to the noise of bells
And chanting, the torches are carried down to the ghats
Where pilgrims gather, with their fragile leaf-baskets
Laden with rose-petals and stephanotis, each candle alight,
Hundreds of brief flames afloat on your rapid current,
How swiftly you carry us away into the night!
Heart's truth is told
In language all can read and understand:
We offer each our sole wavering light to the one river,
Rose-petals, snow-flake, fallen leaf, gone for ever
On your swift flow our fragile garden of dreams!

FIRE

On my hearth a clear flame flickers:
What more secure, familiar, than this
Room built of ever-speeding light?
So swift its motion it seems to stay
Constant, yet nothing still but this steady seeming,
And I, habituate to what appears
Present before these eyes,
This known, unknown familiar place.

Beautiful, flickering, translucent flame,
Blue, and yellow, and bright, and glowing embers
From earth's deep-buried forests return to me here

[309]

Sun's heat and light: love and wisdom
Of what foreknowing holds in one
Moment those green fronds drinking the sun
And an old woman by her autumn fire?

Fire, wild and free, across millennia
You come to me
From carboniferous forests where none ever walked:
What knowledge of beginnings and endings
Carries this room and all it holds
After my ending, before my beginning
This moment of the ever-changing never-changing?

You will take this body and scatter its ashes, fire,
Your flickering flames, like Loge's music
At the world's end, blaze
Into such a star as those who send their rays
To comfort us with infinite forgiveness
Of your undoing into unending beginning:
What world's consuming
Sends out that constant light?

Fire, subtle undoer, loosener of bonds,
Free, you are the freer
Of all that is destructible, perishable, but we
By flame cannot be burned, nor can you consume away
The intangible thought I offer you in praise
As you roar in glory through houses and worlds and universes
Turning our dust to stars.

MEMORY OF SARNATH

For Marco Pallis

IT was the face, they say, of the Enlightened One
Recalled his first disciples, unconvinced
By words, whose countenance
Blissful as life and calm as death, tells all

And nothing to generations of our kind.
Carved in wood, or stone, or cast in bronze,
Silver or gold, great civilizations have adorned
With all the treasures of the soul
That plenitude of emptiness, that known unknown,
The unknown known all know and are. That Prince
Who fled by night his palaces and gardens
Fathomed our mystery, whose only scripture is a smile
All read, and know its doctrine to be true:
Being itself, unbounded as the stars.

A HEAD OF PARVATI

Parvati, whose likeness dreaming hands have wrought
From dried clay of India, who are you, whence
That beauty, noble and peaceful face of love?
Whose that serene presence, present
Here in my room? From what mind, what thought
That aspect of beautitude? Whose love? For whom?
Mystery of love we both receive and give,
That goddess-face comes from high and far
Still mountain lake reflecting
Clouds, storms, stars, silences, night – her native place.

LONDON DAWN

Mornings – how gladly I return
From inner lands, unknown
Houses, rooms, journies, prisons,
Regions where terror takes form of bridge or parapet,
Gulf, precipice, swollen river, to wake again
Into this world's dawn,
Escape the hells of dream.
We do not choose but must enact
The part the night assigns.

I draw back my curtain
And see the windows of men and women lit,
One by one, human neighbours returning to the known
They for a time call home, as I.
One tends a daisy-bush, green from his fingers, a woman
Watches the two pigeons in the sycamore
That nets the sky with twigs these winter mornings;
A man pulls on a shirt, assumes his role.

Where have they come from? Savage lands,
Neglected gardens, sanctuaries, the embrace
Of love, or of God? Most, I would guess,
Alone, as I am, yet not lonely,
To London bricks and sparrows
Driven by Eumenides
Or by departing angel led each to our place,
Shared day, where we may know and love one another.

NOT IN TIME

I SHALL not return
To dear past places
Or be again
With those who shared my days,

But I will pass
Into lives unborn
Not through these words,
But we who have been

Sing in young hearts, this, this
Is your long-lost love
Whom you have known
Always, through our desire
To gaze on a remembered face.

PARADISE SEED

WHERE is the seed
Of the tree felled,
Of the forest burned,

Or living root
Under ash and cinders?
From woven bud

What last leaf strives
Into life, last
Shrivelled flower?

Is fruit of our harvest,
Our long labour
Dust to the core?

To what far, fair land
Borne on the wind
What winged seed

Or spark of fire
From holocaust
To kindle a star?

NO WHERE

THERE is a place
More real than here
That is no where.

From regions of memory
Boundless joy
Opens its distances,

Regions of loss
Vast as love, high
As heart aspires.

Far, far
And wide as absence
Those groves and fields,

Long as departure
Its rivers flow
Beyond hope's reach.

Realms of elsewhere
Whose time is once,
Whose place is away

In long-ago gardens
Those bird voices
Sing of our loves

That never were,
Yet deep as life,
Yet all that we are.

THE DREAM

WHAT land is native to us but a dream
We have told one another, leaf by leaf,
Golden bough and golden flower,
Fountain and tree and stream,
That Paradise unseen.

Its unheard music we have sung
Lover to lover,
In sunlit glades we have depicted Her,
Our Eve, our Primavera,
And sweet Virgin Mary with all her babes,

Whose bliss is ours – not that our fingers played
With strand of golden hair
Or reached for that ripe fruit
She offers, or lily-flower,
Holy mother to holy child,

But we have made it so –
Those angels, sinless saints,
Souls who, purified by death,
Dwell in our images for ever, neither come
Nor go from that imagined place.

We, who have loved and known
Beauty only as we have traced those presences
Robed and adorned with beyond-price jewels
Of our imagining

Is it that we are
Semblances in the enactment of a dream
That dreams us, life by shadowy life
In Eden, under those bright boughs,
Beside that flowing stream?

ALL THIS

ALL this – a story we have told one another
And in the telling made to be
A world – the Book of Life, raised altar and tower,
Traced lineaments of beauty and power
That stare back at us with deep goddess-eyes,
Or stone regard. We have made them other
To tell ourselves of our loves, our triumphs, our terrors.
Told the thousand-and-one stories to enchant ourselves,
Hold converse with gods, animals, demon-kings,
Dragons, oracular birds and burning mountains,
Fought in the Great Battle, travelled the Desert Journey,
Age-long our quest for the Holy Grail, the Lapis, the Rose-garden.
We have descended into hell, been visited by angels,
Drunk from the fountains.

Temples we have built, stone by inscribed stone,
Eloquent of the heavenly order – how beautiful
Those mirroring mosques, rose-windows onto other worlds,
Dreadful and dire those dead-end streets where the night-lost
Howl our despair's violent insatiable desires,
And oh! the tears we weep
As we declaim our tragedies, line by irretractable line.

Now it seems we can no longer stop
The nightmare, neither wake ourselves nor sleep
Nor save the poor sufferers whose parts we play,
We, the frenzied tellers, the doomed enactors
Of all world's folly and glory,
We, who have seen the Holy Face, the holocaust,
Still must press on to know what happens in the end.

With what splendours and miseries we have amazed ourselves
Shakespeare and Proust have told, and the recording angels,
And the old, who are once and for ever,
Wonder why we did not write a different story –
Too many tears there have been, and too much sorrow,
Yet, as I have turned the pages of my days
Each has unfolded the one mystery, incomprehensible, boundless.

MEMORY-PLACES

MEMORY-PLACES – but not ours
Those flashes of recollection: from what unknown elsewhere
An old wall, the corner of a stair, familiar,
Yet when and where, to whom? For an instant
I was that other's presence there
In a country that is no where, a place
Not vague or shadowy, but clear
As a room painted by Chardin or Vermeer
Or Bonnard's garden, or Sienese balcony
Where angel reflected from an inner heaven

[316]

Communes with virgin reverie.
Oh where are those gardens fragrant with basil and orange-trees
In long-ago cities no archaeologist can disinter
From this world's dust! Once and for ever they are,
Though no path comes or goes, the numberless hours and days
      of the living!

An essence, breath of a life not mine
From a here and now far as stars, light-years away
Whose past reaches our present when they no longer are:
As unshed tears
That sunlit wall, that corner of a stair.

STARLINGS

STARLINGS
In multitude, whence and why
From London sky as to a trysting-place
At evening came to rest outside my house
Like scattered leaves returning to their tree
To raise their wordless chorus:
What will impels them as they carry
Unheeded over doomed cities
Meaning and beauty?
Ignorant of what they are to us
The birds are in their joy.

NATURE CHANGES AT THE SPEED OF LIFE . . .

NATURE changes at the speed of life
From moment to moment, so that all,
Bird, leaf and tree seem still, seem real, until
We glimpse the conjurer at play –
A dandelion's evanescent sphere

[317]

Created itself, between yesterday and today
Came, was, and is over, while I
Marvel at that unseen geometer's skill
Who builds the transcience where we dwell.

SOLILOQUIES

I TRY to understand
The leaves that wave to me in the morning wind,
Beautiful forms the fingers of air
Play with, as they play with my thin hair,
Endlessly kind, the language of nature
Too simple to be read
By such as I.

*

I WAKE to the familiar from the unknown
Dream-places where I also am, as they
Dwindle and submerge; all day
In this familiar room
I have been struggling to climb
A hill of sliding wave-worn stones innumerable:
Who, and where, am I?

*

AND yet I praise
The light I have shadowed,
The good refused,
The truth denied,
The beauty defaced,
The love I have wounded.

*

'IN the destructive element, immerse' –
And the blind leap into the void
Becomes the peace of those who have nothing to lose,
The moment of freedom when all is understood.

*

I SET out in a dream
To go away –
Away is hard to go, but no one
Asked me to stay,
And there is no destination
For away.

*

To make the imperfect perfect
It is enough to love it.

*

WHAT dreamer dreams my life-long quest?
Why must heart soar, and mind
Seek what is high and far?
Travelling a world of wonders have I lost or found
What is dear and near?

*

INCREDIBLE that anything exists – this hotch-potch
World of marvels and trivia, and which is which?

*

I HAVE been
And known profusion
Of wonders, yet remain
Unsatisfied, desiring
Nothing.

*

I PRAISE your splendour,
River of light, joy
Shadowless, that will fade
Me away, like cloud
Into pure sky.

THE TURQUOISE SUNSET . . .

THE turquoise sunset evening sky
Asked, 'Why stay below, for here
Spaces are infinite where angels are
Unbounded from star to star.'

I replied 'Soul builds her house
In the fleeting here and now
Of once and never again for ever –
What do angels know
Of the human ways of sorrow?'

Sky said, 'You will be returning
Soon to where memory gives place
To ever-presence,' and I
'Through lifelong years we love
Dear human faces that must die.'

POPPY-FLOWER

TODAY a wondrous hundredfold poppy
With muddled mauve and crimson petals
Has opened at my garden door in once only
Miraculous epiphany –
And who am I that the creator of numberless worlds
Should send this gift from the inexhaustible treasury?

Today in Persia a mountain shook
Human multitudes with no more concern
Than fallen petals, or stars in galaxies –
And who are we
In that Presence to whom large and small,
Many and one, are alike, are nothing, are all?

ARK

I SEND soul like a dove
Out from this fragile ark
Afloat in space.

Body puts out a hand
And soul's secure again
In time and place.

Into the unknown
Soul ventures her love
To bring back some green leaf.

Into the shoreless dark
Whence none returns
The raven flies.

PRAYER TO THE LORD SHIVA

For Karan Singh

IN this world-storm, under this dark sky
I seek refuge in darkness.
Here where the heart is dead, blood shed
I seek refuge in heart's blood.
In the destroyer
From world's destruction I seek refuge,

From the slaughterer, the wounder
Hide in the wound, from the killer
Claim sanctuary
In death, with all who pray
Beyond mortality
To reach that secret bliss.

WANTING NO LONGER . . .

WANTING no longer those things that from day to day
We hope and fear, what, soul, would you wish might be
If all were possible? What would I,
Who have been given, and spent, a life,
A world, though never enough?
Oh, nothing again of the once only, not for time
To turn back that moving image as it slips away,
Yet I am full of longing, as the unborn
For what will be:
I long for longing, desire desire, hope for hope
That at the end, as at the beginning
Angelic watchers may know what it is we do,
And why, and for the unknown
To show me what I am, and what is love!

LISTEN

'LISTEN,' you say, invisible one,
'You do not hear my wisdom,
Time is too far,
That endless journey away.'

Then shall we meet in death, at the end of time? I answer,
'My last companion?'
But you reply only
'Listen!'

At the back-end of time
Leaf-fall of lives, dwindling of the great tree
To the acorn of forests, returning
To the nothing of all that is,
The seasons, the leaves, the loves,
Song to its source, soul to its star –
Winter's recollection of worlds to be.

PARADOX

For Muriel Bradbrook

Louis, sainted king of France,
Asked a courtier, it is said,
'Do you, at midnight, suffer, ever,
From doubts?' The courtier
Answered, 'Yes.' The saint's reply
More surprising: 'Then you have advanced farther than I
For I have none.'
           Complex paradox –
A saint's certainty respecting the unsure?
Or perhaps royal courtesy?
I, of another time and place
Revolve the facets in my modern mind:
For me it is otherwise, who, at night,
Sink into the everlasting peace
But in broad daylight find
This world incomprehensible, succourless.

AFTER HEARING A RECORDING OF MUSIC BY HILDEGARD OF BINGEN

I HEARD soul singing
In rapturous lonely voice.
Her face only God sees.

Hidden
In the heart of the one
Beloved, as in the evening

A bird alone;
Her song in praise
Of the unknown.

DISSOLVING IDENTITY

As if permeable – it seems
Body no longer bounds my times and places,
Past and future merging in the measureless
Abundance, not much or little, but all –
Mountains, waterfalls, leaves, seas,
Clouds, birds, skies, whatever is,
The marvels or the shabby commonplace
Suffice for the *mysterium* to indwell.

And by more than these
I have known and have been known –
Human, who are you, friends, familiar
Dear companions of home, from the beginning
You have been with me, have come and gone,
Are as myself?
                    Beloved father of my childhood,
Mother, whom I have so deeply known
As if your dreams and longings
Flow in my veins, unbearable,
So much, one blood-drop more
I shall become the world.

DO I IMAGINE REALITY...

Do I imagine reality
Or does the real imagine me?
Unimaginable imaginer
What part does the imagined play?

CHRISTMAS-PRESENT

THE coat my son has given me this Christmas day
I would be wearing in a garden
That once was mine, and still might be
If I were permitted to return
And take another way
Than what has been.
He has given the garment he has seen
As fitting that other place and time
Where he best remembers me.

PETITE MESSE SOLENNELLE

*For my granddaughter Elizabeth,
among the second sopranos*

BROCKLEY, was it, or Ilford, one of the numberless places
Of absence, the church porch overgrown, as in Holman Hunt's
Painting that hung in my father's bedroom long ago,
But there were people, they might have been anyone, anonymous –
You would have thought they could know little of paradise.

I among the listeners looked idly on
As the singers filed in, the young and the middle-aged, women
    and men,

Then they began to sing, and I to wonder
Where I had seen these faces before, faces familiar
In golden Florentine or Roman splendour
Gathered round the Madonna and her haloed child,
Apostles at the Last Supper with their Master,
Transfigured, and angel choirs with bodies of music,
The soul in every face
Made visible, reflecting heaven.

For the face of every soul is beautiful –
In outer suburb, inner city, Rossini's music
As once in Naples, or Bologna, in places and faces of exile
Tracing the hidden lineaments, transient, eternal.

Uncollected & New Poems

WHO LISTENS ...

WHO listens, when in the concert-hall,
   The great whispering-gallery
Vaulted ear of the encaverned god
Scattered in our multitude
Ebb and flow the waves of the world?
In deep ocean weed
Sways, like a caress,
Life's delicate responsive cilia.
Sound passes like air
Over a field of grass, whose thousand ears
Bend to the wind, to the oracular voice
Ten thousand auricles attend
As the one hearer hears in all.

Published in The New Yorker in the 1940s.
Set to music by Marshall Bialosky, 1981

ON A SHELL-STREWN BEACH

WHAT are you looking for,
Hoping to find there
On the sea shore?
      A marvellous shell
      More bright than rainbow
      Small as a pearl
      And carved like the tower
      Of a white cathedral.

What are you waiting for,
Tide after tide
On the shore of the ocean?
      I have come seeking

The infinite cipher
And sum of all wisdom
Inscribed on a grain
Of sand that can lie
In the palm of my hand.

Have you searched in vain,
Waited in vain
On the white beaches?
By every tide
The white strand
Is strewn with treasure,
Shells without number
Brighter than rainbow
Formed in pools
Deeper than dreams
In purple water
That teems with creation,
I have found
A myriad particles
And each is all
That can ever be told,
But all are inscribed
With a signature
That I cannot read,
Nor may I inhabit
Their towers of ivory
And golden houses.

The Listener,
13 September, 1951

DESCENT INTO HADES

INSTANTLY they are about me, presences
In multitude, invisible they surround, press
Close at heart: 'Tell, tell,' they say, 'tell
The untold of buried hearts that cannot rest
Till emptied of all that through the dark blood flowed
And pale tears shed.
Our sorrow lives in you, sorrow and love
Untellable, untold. Tell, tell,' they say,
'Tell our secret who, unsatisfied,
Inhabit now your heart, you who must speak
The love we bore, the love we bear in you,
In you, who must remember us, remember for us
Who did not know our hearts, when there were days,
Days when we might have given you our love
Who would not know our hidden truth, now yours,
Our life your life,
Sorrow uncomforted and love unspoken;
And you must love us now
With our rejected loves that love on now in you,
Bound in the bonds of pain,
Of pain we caused,
Cause of the only pain the dead can know,
Who suffer us, who are at your mercy
As you at ours.'

Now they are silent: they attend within
The writing of this page of life for them in blood
That gives them speech: my blood, my speech
I pour into their open pit, my chthonic heart.
Their flesh put off, I know them life to life,
Who am their life, they mine to the end of time,
My time which they bequeathed me to inhabit,
Whose lengthening years full circle turn
Back to the heart where they await.
I would beg my dead for mercy,
To bless with all their powerless wisdom, speechless grace,

Be blessed by them, and find beatitude
For them, and for myself, and for my children,
Who are their children, are their ancestors;
But not yet is heart's fill of sorrow shed
Whose tortuous veins bind us, dead and living, pain to pain.

ORACLES

FROM their grave lion-mouths, oracles
With angel-tongues outpour
Continuous the silent flood of time.
But we who cannot stem, but are that flow
Known only that we fall and fall
From source to abyss for ever.
Their serene wisdom is the book of life we write
In blood and ignorance, who are
Incomprehensible utterance of masks of dream.

THE CHARTRES ANNUNCIATION

No, that carved angel whose still smile
The sun reveals or shadow veils
Day and night through centuries
Is not her lover, towards whom she bends
Attentive, as he towards her inclines.
To her solitude he brings
His silent telling of world to world.
Flesh that from flesh conceives ignores
The mystery of god from god;
That angel-smile in sun-warmed stone
Intelligence of dream imparts,
Her mystery in whose human house
All children are the divine child.

MY FATHER'S BIRTHDAY

15 March 1880

HE remained silent on many things,
In his last years, he could not speak of
To wife or daughter who had never shared
Memories and hopes nearest his heart. Only with children
  he could
Share the simplicity of receiving from God
With gladness what each day brought,
The morning sun, the task he never refused.
His month was windy March, when coltsfoot flowers
Open their bright disks to receive the sun, or close
Against the chill and cloud of a harsh season.
On my childhood my father shone like an early sun,
Who in his old age closed his rays against the cold
Climate of a loveless house.

TO THE SUN

1

SUN, great giver of all that is,
Once more I return from dream to your times and places
As geese wing over London in this morning's dawn
Before the human city invades your immaculate spaces.
Sun, greatest of givers, your speeding rays
Weave again familiar quotidian things, epiphanies
Of trees, leaves, wings, jewelled rain, shining wonders.
Your golden mask covers the unknown
Presence of the awakener of all eyes
On whose blinding darkness none can gaze.
Clouds and hills and gardens and forests and seas,
High-rise buildings, dust and ordure, derelict and broken things
Receive alike from holiest, purest source

Meaning and being, messages each morning brings
To this threshold where I am.
Old, I marvel that I have been, have seen
Your everything and nothing realm, all-giving sun.

2

How address you, greatest of givers,
God, angel, these words served once, but no longer
Apollo's chariot or Surya's horses imaged in stone
Of Konarak, glorious metaphor of the advancing power
Of the unwearied sun from the eternal East. My time
Has other symbols, speeding light waves, light-years, rays
Cycling for ever the boundless sphere of space,
Vast emptiness of what is or is not,
Unsolid matter's equivocal seeming –
Science only another grandiose myth we have dreamed,
Ptolemaic or Copernican, or Einstein's paradigm
Less real than those magnificent stone horses
As light triumphs over darkness for yet one more day.
But no myth, as before our eyes you are, or seem!
In your numinous glory I have seen you rise
From beyond the Farne Isles casting your brilliance
Over cold northern seas, or over the seas of Greece,
Have seen you great rim rising from India's ocean.
As you circle the earth birds sing your approach each morning,
New flowers open in wilderness, gardens, waste-places,
All life your retinue, as before all eyes you summon,
Greatest of givers, your heavens outspread
Our earth's vast and minute spaces, to each the whole,
And today I receive yet again from your inexhaustible treasury
Of light, this room, this green garden, my boundless universe.

3

Ancestral sun, do you remember us,
Children of light, who behold you with living eyes?
Are we as you, are you as we? It seems
As if you look down on us with living face:

Who am I who see your light but the light I see,
Held for a moment in the form I wear, your beams.

I have stood on shores of many seas,
Of lakes and rivers, and always over the waters,
Across those drowning gulfs of fear
Your golden path has come to me
Who am but one among all who depart and return.

Blinding sun, with your corona of flames, your chasms of fire,
Presence, terrible theophany,
Am I in you, are you in me,
Infinite centre of your unbounded realm
Whose multitudes sing Holy, Holy, Holy?
Do you go into the dark, or I?

4

Not that light is holy, but that the holy is the light –
Only by seeing, by being, we know,
Rapt, breath stilled, bliss of the heart.
No microscope nor telescope can discover
The immeasurable: not in the seen but in the seer
Epiphany of the commonplace.
A hyacinth in a glass it was, on my working-table,
Before my eyes opened beyond beauty light's pure living flow.
'It is I,' I knew, 'I am that flower, that light is I,
'Both seer and sight.'
Long ago, but for ever; for none can un-know
Native Paradise in every blade of grass,
Pebble, and particle of dust, immaculate.
'It has been so and will be always,' I knew,
No foulness, violence, ignorance of ours
Can defile that sacred source:
Why should I, one of light's innumerable multitude,
Fear in my unbecoming to be what for ever is?

TESTIMONY

So late, for whom, to whom
Do I speak, for the old, for the young,
Of for no-one? To none
Of these – from the everlasting to the unborn, undying
I speak, who am alone
In a time and place where none
Will find me, who am already gone,
When you, whoever you may be,
Old, young, in the middle of life's way
Are with me in this no-place, no-time
Unbounded, where each is, who for a moment holds,
As I now, in your heart, the world.
As you I am
Heart's cup, filled for a moment
From ocean and air and light,
This body, this cup that overflows
With the one Presence, will be gone,
Dissolved again, as again and again
Drop in the ocean,
Will have become you, no more
This woman whose hand writes words not mine,
Bequeathed by multitude of the once living
Who knew, loved, understood and told
Meanings passed down
To the yet to come, whose faces I shall not see,
Yet whom as I write these words, I already am.

I BELIEVE NOTHING . . .

I BELIEVE nothing – what need
Surrounded as I am with marvels of what is,
This familiar room, books, shabby carpet on the floor,
Autumn yellow jasmine, crysanthemums, my mother's flower,

[336]

Earth-scent of memories, daily miracles,
Yet media-people ask, 'Is there a God?'
What does the word mean
To the fish in his ocean, birds
In his skies, and stars?

I only know that when I turn in sleep
Into the invisible, it seems
I am upheld by love, and what seems is
Inexplicable here and now of joy and sorrow,
This inexhaustible, untidy world –
I would not have it otherwise.

CONFESSIONS

WANTING to know all
I overlooked each particle
Containing the whole
Unknowable.

*

INTENT on one great love, perfect,
Requited and for ever,
I missed love's everywhere
Small presence, thousand-guised.

*

AND lifelong have been reading
Book after book, searching
For wisdom, but bringing
Only my own understanding.

*

FORGIVE me, forgiver,
Whether you be infinite omniscient
Or some unnoticed other
My existence has hurt.

BEING what I am
What could I do but wrong?
Yet love can bring
To heart healing
To chaos meaning.

BABYLON

NOT in vain
This city where lost souls
Hide and seek themselves –
Great building-site of illusion
Here and now always in us
The divine for the divine seeking.

A BLESSING

SOME think me wise
Generous and kind –
May that image bless
Your need, your distress.

Others see a destroyer –
May that dread aspect
You hate and fear
Warn from the abyss.

I am a mask of God
Among his myriadfold
Who turns to you my face
Who am no-one, no-where.

ASSASSIN

THE assassin is someone you already know, near
At hand, not at heart, even though you assume you are fond of,
But your soul is not; you prefer to lie to yourself
If you think they too are deceived
By the falseness of the less than love
That eases daily intercourse.
Side by side you hide your evasions, you forget
(But they do not) that moment of truth between you,
And when Brutus' knife falls, is Caesar every really surprised?
Ideologies that seeming friend nurses, who hides
Those other values from you in your presence,
Or with whom it is easier to agree to differ, but not really –
At the moment of fame, of success, of the world's praise
When we think our friends will be glad, it is not so:
The assassin is hidden in your shadow, and this you know.

HOPE IS TO CREATE . . .

HOPE is to create
In possibility
What for ever is
Heart's mystery,

Therefore I hope for hope,
Desire desire
That brings our seed to flower
To fire our fire.

SIN OF OMISSION . . .

Sin of omission: as women
Withhold love, so I
Poetry, perpetual praise,
Sound of the universe,
Song without words
Unheard, unsung.

GARDEN SIMURGH

I hung out nuts for the blue-tits but the sparrows came,
All thirty of them
With flurry of wings,
One mind in thirty vociferous selves,
Each cheerfully affirming its birdism unique, as perhaps it is
In a certain sense.
                    Why then
My discontent, my looking for something else,
The blue-tits who have not come, my dissatisfaction
At having bought a wire feeder with perches and a bag of nuts
Just for sparrows, for whom bread-crusts would have done as well –
But why not for these
Survival-of-the-fittest cheerful Londoners, who knew William Blake,
What wonder-bird was I looking for? How are peacock or nightingale
Not to say Sri Aurobindo's super-bird, more miraculous
Than these two-a-farthing sparrows
Each feather bearing the carelessly-worn signature
Of the universe that has brought them here to the Lord's table
With such delight, never doubting their welcome?

HOW CAN I...

How can I or my kind know what to hope
At the end of what has been?
Is it for us
To oppose what was in the beginning,
Our incarnation of the divine
Unknown terrible creator?
We who enter the fire
Rise with the flames, whither?

DREAM-WORDS

SILENT world of seas, mountains, rivers,
Swamps, precipices, dangerous
Paths, silent people; but when words
Are uttered, who speaks these phrases
Laden with meaning
That as we return to morning, fades?

HOUSELESS HOPE...

For M. Selim-ur-Rahman

HOUSELESS hope, houseless hope
Be my thought as you take your course
From the source
To the end of days, be mine
For this time and place.

Houseless love, houseless love
Shelter in my heart as you pass
Through the world, seeking
Your beloved, your homecoming
In this night of time.

Joy, bird with no place of alighting, fly
Through my sky's
Infinite space's, boundless
Realms of delight,
At rest in flight.

SHORT POEMS 1994

AGAINST the *nihil*
One candle-flame, one blade of grass,
One thought suffices
To affirm all.

*

TIME to unknow
What has been known,
Time to undo
What has been done –
What will remain?
The naked soul
To judgement come.

*

DOWN from God in heaven –
The human city
Has come to this
Great cry of heartbreak, utterance
Of joy that seeks to be,
That will not die.

*

OLD I no longer suffer –
Ash from the fire:
Does any grain
Of gold remain?

*

ALL I have known and been
I bequeath to whoever
Can decipher my poem.

*

SPRING returns to the old
Not flowers but memories
Rising from earth
In rebirth.

*

DEAR friends elsewhere
I shall not see again,
Sun's light unites us, and the air,
And the one thought
Of the world we share.

*

So far, so good,
And when pain comes
I talk to God.

BIRD-PALACES

EMPTY air –
Then one of the myriad seeds
Of the tree of life fell in my London garden,
Opened its cotyledons, sent roots down,
And a young tree there
Opened its spaces,
Creating times and places
For birds whose nature
Delights in branches
Where winds stir

Slender leaf, heavy flowers.
Wood pigeon, blackbird and robin trace
Invisible bird-palaces in the air.

I SEE MY LITTLE CAT . . .

I SEE my little cat sleeping in her favourite chair,
Her world unquestioned and secure,
And know I will be gone, and wonder where
She will find a different chair, and will she remember
The games we played: 'Is pussy coming to bed?' and
    'Scamper-scamper!'
And dashing before me to behind the bedroom door
Hidden and crouching ready to pounce
When my slow steps arrive, and I say 'Well done
Little pussy!' and give her her supper on a saucer
While I turn down my bed; and our morning play
'Come, pussy, down the garden!' and watch her tear
Up the acacia tree where the pigeons are
And a squirrel sometimes, and wonder whether
She will remember my voice, and wonder
Why her world has disappeared, or with nimble paws
Leap lightly from here to there, secure.
I hope she will not mourn me, or not for long.

LEGENDARY KINGS

For the birthday of HRH The Prince of Wales
14 November 1997

IN time immemorial those sacred kings
Traced their lineage to the Sun god, the God Sun
In his great chariot of the living:

Elephants, nagas, flute-players, dancers, lovers
All spun from the living light that circles the years and days
Of all who have been, are, or will be begotten,

Generations of teeming earth and air and spawn of ocean –
Being, consciousness and bliss their heritage.

Crowned and adorned with magical ornaments
They understood the language of birds, obeyed the oracles,
Learned from the book of life, whose leaves are forests,

Their kingdoms without history, their laws
Attuned to the harmony of the stars and planets
They lived the unending poem written by God,

Assumed and enacted their destined parts,
Scattered the golden pollen-dust of glory,
Seed of imagined cities, embodiments of our dreams,
Building in hope, falling in ruin, yet they have been,

Or will be, and we, remembering
All world's love and suffering, endurance, failure and aspiration
Wonder, and weep, and rejoice.

FOR DAVID GASCOYNE, FALLEN SILENT

WHEN you fell silent, David, spirit,
Come to this place where we walk in darkness,
Dwelling in Hades, could find no voice
To tell of the golden heavens, our native place.
Chattering shadows of shadows,
Mechanisms with inhuman utterance,
Meaningless, confuse us in this post-real world.
You came to bring a message, but fallen on this hard ground
Hurt and wingless,
Inaudible your speech of angels.
Yet in the deep of our night,
Empty of all that love has lost,

Ignorance denied, destroyed, you tell us,
This is the tomb
Where the holy deathless one lies
In every heart awaiting resurrection:
Eloquent your silence to the lonely listener
For the still, small voice of the divine.

From Temenos Academy Review,
Spring 1999

MILLENNIAL HYMN TO
THE LORD SHIVA

1

EARTH no longer
Hymns the Creator,
The seven days of wonder,
The Garden is over –
All the stories are told,
The seven seals broken
All that begins
Must have its ending,
Our striving, desiring,
Our living and dying,
For Time, the bringer
Of abundant days
Is Time the destroyer –
   In the Iron Age
   The Kali Yuga
   To whom can we pray
   At the end of an era
   But the Lord Shiva,
   The Liberator, the purifier?

OUR forests are felled,
Our mountains eroded,
The wild places
Where the beautiful animals
Found food and sanctuary
We have desolated,
A third of our seas,
A third of our rivers
We have polluted
And the sea-creatures dying.
Our civilisation's
Blind progress
In wrong courses
Through wrong choices
Has brought us to nightmare
Where what seems,
Is, to the dreamer,
The collective mind
Of the twentieth century –
This world of wonders
Not divine creation
But a big bang
Of blind chance,
Purposeless accident,
Mother Earth's children,
Their living and loving,
Their delight in being
Not joy but chemistry,
Stimulus, reflex,
Valueless, meaningless,
While to our machines
We impute intelligence,
In computers and robots
We store information
And call it knowledge,
We seek guidance

By dialling numbers,
Pressing buttons,
Throwing switches,
In place of family
Our companions are shadows,
Cast on a screen,
Bodiless voices, fleshless faces,
Where was the Garden
A Disneyland
Of virtual reality,
In place of angels
The human imagination
Is peopled with footballers
Filmstars, media-men,
Experts, know-all
Television personalities,
Animated puppets
With cartoon faces –
　　To whom can we pray
　　For release from illusion,
　　From the world-cave,
　　But Time the destroyer,
　　The liberator, the purifier?

3

THE curse of Midas
Has changed at a touch,
A golden handshake
Earthly paradise
To lifeless matter,
Where once was seed-time,
Summer and Winter,
Food-chain, factory farming,
Monocrops for supermarkets,
Pesticides, weed-killers
Birdless springs,
Endangered species,

Battery-hens, hormone injections,
Artificial insemination,
Implants, transplants, sterilization,
Surrogate births, contraception,
Cloning, genetic engineering, abortion,
And our days shall be short
In the land we have sown
With the Dragon's teeth
Where our armies arise
Fully armed on our killing-fields
With land-mines and missiles,
Tanks and artillery,
Gasmasks and body-bags,
Our aircraft rain down
Fire and destruction,
Our spacecraft broadcast
Lies and corruption,
Our elected parliaments
Parrot their rhetoric
Of peace and democracy
While the truth we deny
Returns in our dreams
Of Armageddon,
The death-wish, the arms-trade,
Hatred and slaughter
Profitable employment
Of our thriving cities,
The arms-race
To the end of the world
Of our postmodern, post-Christian,
Post-human nations,
Progress to the nihil
Of our spent civilisation.
But cause and effect,
Just and inexorable
Law of the universe
No fix of science,
Nor amenable god

Can save from ourselves
The selves we have become,
We are all in it,
No one is blameless –
   At the end of history
   To whom can we pray
   But to the destroyer,
   The liberator, the purifier?

4

IN the beginning
The stars sang together
The cosmic harmony,
But Time, imperceptible
Taker-away
Of all that has been,
All that will be,
Our heart-beat your drum,
Our dance of life
Your dance of death
In the crematorium,
Our high-rise dreams,
Valhalla, Utopia,
Xanadu, Shangri-la, world revolution
Time has taken, and soon will be gone
Cambridge, Princeton and M.I.T.,
Nalanda, Athens and Alexandria
All for the holocaust
Of civilisation –
   To whom shall we pray
   When our vision has faded
   But the world-destroyer,
   The liberator, the purifier?

5

BUT great is the realm
Of the world-creator,
The world-sustainer
From whom we come,
In whom we move
And have our being,
About us, within us
The wonders of wisdom,
The trees and the fountains,
The stars and the mountains,
All the children of joy,
The loved and the known,
The unknowable mystery
To whom we return
Through the world-destroyer –
   Holy, holy
   At the end of the world
   The purging fire
   Of the purifier, the liberator!

From Resurgence No. 197, 1999

Index of titles and first lines

(Titles are set in italic, first lines in roman.)